The Tolerance Law

A Novel

Ashley Baker

The Inkwell Press
Houston, Texas

The Inkwell Press
— Est. 2023 —

Copyright © 2023 by Ashley Baker.
All rights reserved.

Published in the United States by The Inkwell Press, Houston, Texas.

Paperback ISBN 9798376708460

Printed in the United States of America
First printing 2023

Cover Design by Lauren George of Arete Graphix
Author photography: Amanda Faucett Photography

The Tolerance Law is a work of fiction. Names, characters, places, and incidents are the product of the author's imagination or are used fictitiously. Any resemblance to actual events, locales, or persons, living or dead, is entirely coincidental.

To Mark

I

The Outlands

1

"On this day, the thirteenth of December, the Tolerance Law shall be enacted. Henceforth, there shall no longer be any covenants, marriages, or unions due to the nature of exclusion. Tolerance is law." Marjorie Shaw, the principal military advisor, furrowed her brow. Loudspeakers projected her speech in the Outlands. A listening crowd moved closer as a bitter wind howled around them. The cold and barren land held up a gray sky.

"Hate crimes of affection toward only one individual are strictly prohibited. Citizens of Eliora must show equal love to all. Equality, egalitarian economics, matrilineal clans, and matrilocal living arrangements are our future." Armed, black-uniformed Nomarchs lined the stage, looking out at the shivering crowd through gas masks. The Bromley family stood together. Evander's fists clenched. Mari, his wife, stood next to him. They both glanced down at their one child, nine-year-old Nova.

Officer Shaw stiffened. Her voice hardened, "The final solution of The Tolerance Law shall span fifteen years: all male offspring below the age of two, as well as any future male produced under these hateful conditions, will be discarded as the Matriarchy is instated. This law is effective immediately, under penalty of death. Tolerance is law. Spread no more hate."

A voice was heard in the Outlands—the cry of a mother who refused to be comforted because she knew her one-and-a-half-year-old son would be no more. Nomarchs dragged the woman away. Her feet trailed through the snow. Nova squeezed her mother's hand. With her other hand, she nervously rubbed her gloved fingers together.

Two flickering screens on either side of Officer Shaw's podium flickered to life. Nova's head tilted at the contrast between the icy Outlands and The Fractal City of Eliora that came onto the screen. The sun shone between the high-rise buildings. On the screen, the Vizier's appointed Thought Leaders nailed The Tolerance Law onto the doors of a gutted cathedral. Nomarchs had already removed all the red fabric pews, and the stained-glass windows hid behind planks, all boarded up.

In the middle of The Fractal City of Eliora, cameras flashed, capturing shots of the Vizier smiling as she posed for the media with her Thought Leaders outside the cathedral's doors. The camera lens framed Ida Watt's silky ash-brown hair that fell just past her tight, drawn-in shoulders. The gutted cathedral and a picturesque cityscape filled the rest of the shot. The camera's loud click-chunk made Outlanders shutter.

Eliora's leader projected a self-important grin. Ambitious for the tolerance that would bring everyone under her influence, the Vizier lifted her hand and waved.

Nova adjusted her wool-felt hat, pushing her golden hair behind her ear as she watched. Two other children moved closer. The boy whispered to Nova, "What did she say?"

"Shhhh..." Mari held a finger to her lips in a motherly manner. "Don't let the Nomarchs hear you." She pulled the children closer as the biting wind continued to blow. Despite being surrounded by her two friends and family, Nova's head pounded at the Vizier's words,

"Come out of the horrifying thickets that hedge you in. Do more than believe. Live your freedom and put it on display. Our battle is not over until you practice equality at school, work, home, and in our streets.

Live your freedom!"

2

Two years after Vizier Ida Watts enacted the Tolerance Law, Mari Bromley gave birth to her son. A biting wind blew around the Bromley family outside the Outland's birth center. Because Mari had not reported her pregnancy, she missed the mandatory gender reveal ultrasound.

"This could have ended quietly if you would have complied," a Medical Nomarch rebuked Mari. "Now look at the scene you are making." Black boots strode forward quickly as the Nomarchs herded the Bromleys along the frigid riverfront. Nova dreaded the waiting crowd. The noise made her short of breath.

"Stay close," Mari whispered firmly, grasping Nova's hand. "No matter what happens..." Mari's eyes turned to her daughter, "I love you." Nova's head hung between her shoulders as she walked beside her parents. Their feet sloshed through sleet. Water in the Odalys River splashed against icy banks as people streamed beside it in droves. Hundreds of city people surged out of the dome and down the Ouland's pathway—each hoping for a better view of the couple who had broken The Tolerance Law. Voices from the crowd surrounded the Bromleys, humming with electricity. The gas-masked crowd swirled and buzzed with energy. Nova could almost hear the high voltage zinging through them. Grown women giggled like school girls. Daughters mimicked their mothers. Only the elderly moved slowly, seemingly rooted in the ground.

Nomarchs separated Nova's family from the crowd, pushing them onto a dock with weathered wooden planks.

"I love you, sweet baby," Mari mouthed. Her soft eyes glanced at the baby swaddled in a blue blanket. Mari's light pink dress swayed under her fur jacket as she shifted weight from one foot to another. Nova's father, Evander, placed one arm around Mari. He shared prolonged eye contact with his wife. Mari bit her lip and steadied her feet against the ice on the boards. A sea of faces bobbed, trying to get a better view of the baby.

"I want to go home," Nova whispered to her mother. A small cloud of breath exhaled. Nova's chin quivered. She wished she could go home and hide her baby brother, but the watching crowd held the family in its clutches. Mari pulled Nova closer.

"Go," Officer Shaw pointed to the edge of the landing. The crowd erupted in applause. Hands clapped. Feet stomped. The excitement was palpable. At the edge of the pier, a circular wheel with an ornate six-pointed star awaited them. Six different colors and six different fates marked the points of the star.

"The wheel of fortune," Nova shuddered. She remembered hearing about it months earlier when she stood with her friends Emma and Alister. The children listened to the Vizier's decree, "*Live your freedom!*"

"Spin it!" Gawkers in the crowd brought Nova back to her senses. "Spin it," they cried out as if they were both the jury and the judge. Officer Shaw stiffened under her green beret and commander's uniform.

"I present to you the Bromley Family," she yelled, getting the people's attention. Open-armed, she presented them. "They have broken The Tolerance Law."

"Bigot," a man yelled from the crowd.

"Intolerant," a woman echoed.

Nova knew The Tolerance Law annulled her parents' marriage. Her dad could still enter a walking relationship with any woman, including her mother. But when the law was enacted, a Nomarch relocated Evander into his mother's home across the city. Bed chambers were open in every multigenerational matriarchal house, but Evander could only visit his wife at night and had to return to his home before sunrise. The problem was no one was allowed only one partner, and everybody knew they were monogamous. The little boy in his mother's arms changed everything. Out of the crowd's murmur arose a unified chant:

Great Wheel of Fortune
Turn, Turn, Turn,
Tell Them the Lesson
That They Should Learn

The wheel of fortune rumbled, and the game of chance began. No skill could determine the outcome. Nova watched men waving money, frantically trying to place their bets.

Nova grimaced. She knew the six fates by heart. Evander stepped forward, forced to spin the wheel. Under the strength of his right arm, the wheel whizzed around. Colors blurred as it reverberated. Time slowed down. In a sea of familiar faces, Nova felt like she stood alone.

Despite the cold, Nova's temperature rose as she tried not to think about each fate. Collectively, the crowd drew in a breath. Mari clutched her son when the circular wheel drummed to a stop.

"Orange!" Marjorie Shaw announced. "The ordeal of the basket."
Mari sank to her knees. Evander lunged at a Nomarch. Officer Shaw struck Evander's face with the butt of her gun and cursed loudly at him.

"Get back! Her teeth clenched. The Nomarch turned to Mari and took the newborn from her arms.

"Nova, get behind me," Mari pulled her daughter back. Nova's ankles felt locked in place.

"Why can't I move?" Nova's mind swirled, and her eyes darted, searching her mother's face for answers. Emotionless, the guard stripped Nova's newborn brother and laid him in a basket.

"I present you with a jar of milk," a Nomarch poured the jar over the baby's body.

"A bottle of honey," another Nomarch held up the jug and filled the bottom of the basket with a sticky layer. Nova's mind snapped a bleak picture of her brother: Arms flailing, eyes squinting, mouth squared, and a tiny cry.

Mari covered her mouth. Her whole body shook. Not permitted to leave, she and Evander watched the little basket sail into the open river. It was such a cold day that bugs didn't swarm, but Nova knew the breeze would chill him to the bone. Soon, the baby would no longer cry. But how long would it take for the lethargic and shivering baby to die?

3

Gunshots resounded. The river splashed under the weight of two bodies. Empty shells chinked as they fell onto the dock's wooden planks.

"Mom!" Nova cried, "Dad!" She couldn't see anything after that. Eyes blurring, she blinked tears. Everything moved in slow motion as a Nomarch led her away. All sound faded except the pounding of her own heart in her ears. Her mind captured each moment: the crowd roaring, fists raised in the air, stomping feet.

"Is marriage worth it?" a Nomarch asked loudly. Another officer grabbed Nova's arm and pushed her forward. A hollow numbness enveloped Nova. Her fingertips tingled.

"How is this real?" The corners of her mouth drew downward. At the threshold of the dock, winter's fog weaved its way around her feet. She stood in the moment, but the haze made her feel just behind or ahead of it, not in it. Nova's mind was somewhere else entirely.

Head tilted, she faced the gray sky. She breathed deeply as if the spinning world paused in some unknown universe. Tomorrow, the sun would rise again tomorrow and stretch its rays from east to west. She would feel its warmth again, but not today.

"My family," her lips tightened. Behind her, the river's breath formed a fog that rose to catch a glimpse of the girl driven away. Rocks lining the path nearly cried out. Clouds gathered. The wind howled. A snow-covered thorn stuck out of a dried-up and frozen hedge and scraped Nova's arm as she passed. She pressed her hand over the wound. She felt warm blood ooze between her fingers. Of all the things, why did a thorn make her want to sob?

"My family," Nova staggered forward; a seed of longing fell into her heart. The ache budded with every step. The loss took root in everything she knew. She did not know it yet, but she would never quite feel settled in the Outlands again.

A black snake slithered through the dust into the dense row of dried-up shrubs as a Nomarch turned the key in an iron gate. Stepping into exile, she knew no people, place, or time would be her home. Nova was homesick for a place she did not know.

4

The Outlands orphanage sat in the middle of a frozen wasteland. The six children's homes each had two stories and one door. Nova lived in barrack number five, or *The House of Rats*. Most mornings she saw a rodent scurry across the floor, along with her friends, when the 4 a.m. alarm blasted. In the barrack, thirty-six bunk beds formed a line across the floor. The beds looked lice-laden or infested with some kind of bed bugs.

"Showers every tenth day," the Nomarch stated upon Nova's arrival at the orphanage. A gust of wind seeped through the sides of the unheated bunkhouse. The dirty floors held up gray walls with tinted windows.

"In The House of Rats, you will say 'we' instead of 'I.' The speaker looked into Nova's eyes, "Change your pronouns." Nova held eye contact, but the odor of a latrine bucket made Nova feel like a caged animal. Worse than the smell, though, was the fact that none of the Nomarchs addressed her as a human.

They didn't call her by name but simply spoke to peck instructions into her brain, "022687 say, we swear. We will. We promise," Nomarchs taught the girls to strip off their individuality and to think of themselves as a group. Nova hated their beady eyes, always watching her. They stole every shred of privacy. Nova lived under the Nomarchs' ever-present eye.

"In The Fractal City, illegitimate children won't exist anymore. Your dad should have supported that," a Nomarch pecked the insult.

"Your mom should have known that women can experience gender fairness and territorial expansion. She could have had her own matriarchal home one day," another Nomarch added. "But look what she chose for you with her narrow-minded thinking."

"And no matriarchal grandmother has access to her own grandchildren if her adult children have broken The Tolerance Law." Nova thought, knowing what he'd say next.

"Tolerance. Tolerance. Tolerance." Their iron beaks chipped away day by day until Nova groaned. If the Nomarchs ever saw a tear fall down Nova's cheek, they cocked their heads back and laughed.

Many nights, Nova curled up in bed, thinking, "There is no reason to this place." It was maddening. She wondered if every guard agreed to wave goodbye to common sense when they suited up. What happened to human decency? Would they take every bit of family, health, and happiness?

Most nights, Nova lay in bed with questions swirling. Her prayers seemed to fall on deaf ears. God felt distant and, at moments, completely absent.

"Why?" Nova's throat tightened. "Why my family?" she wiped her cheek, but the tears came anyway. Nova envisioned her mom's pink dress and remembered her final words, "Get behind me." Nova blinked her swollen eyes. They grew so heavy.

Around midnight, Nova's eyes snapped open. She looked around, searching for the crying baby, but the room was dark and quiet.

The dock. The wheel. The basket. Her baby brother's cry. The memory flooded her consciousness. Death is silence. Nova's heart pounded. A cold sweat covered her.

"My brother," she ran her hands through her hair. A tremor overtook her. She lay down. Her lips trembled.

The bunkbed creaked. Nova felt a hand on her back. Nova's bunkmate climbed up and sat next to her.

"I'm here." Emma wrapped an arm around her, barely allowing herself to breathe. Nova would never forget that night. Emma sat beside her with the same fate, yet sensing her distress, she tilted her head to the side and whispered, "I'm here." Nova's heart swelled with emotion when she heard her voice—maybe it was how Emma's face mirrored everything so clearly—the sickness, loss, and loneliness. Nova sighed, letting out a breath slowly.

"This will keep you warm." Emma pulled a blanket over Nova's trembling legs, "Do you want some water?" Something about the tone and care in Emma's voice made a lump grow in the back of Nova's throat. Cup in hand, Nova looked at the pale-faced girl sitting on her bed and rethought everything about her life.

"I'm here to listen— when you're ready." Emma's smile tightened, and she said nothing further. And that was the best thing she could have done, for Nova simply needed a friend. Nova rested her head on Emma's shoulder. Her eyes and nose were red, and Emma stayed with her until she fell asleep. In the days to come, even if Emma became irritable from insufficient sleep or because the soup rations ran low, Nova knew Emma would be family—the sister she never had.

5

The following day, black-suited Nomarchs patrolled the Outlands orphanage. When the 4 a.m. alarm blasted, feet jumped out of bed and scrambled to a snow-littered courtyard. A chilly wind blew.

"It's so cold," Emma said, chin quivering.

"Yeah, we're turning into popsicles." Nova's long blonde hair fell around her face as she walked. The sharp wind cut through her jacket.

The overcast sky veiled the landscape. A Nomarch flipped the floodlights on.

"They look like lemurs in those gasmasks." Nova's lips twisted. "They can't even see. It's like they aren't even human." Nova waved her dog tag in front of a silver pole. Scanning, it chimed. Half-melted snow dotted the cobblestone courtyard.

"Orphan #104352," Count started. Arms hung. Every eye faced forward.

"Here." A Nomarch checked the box by Leena Brown's number on his device.

Six houses surrounded the hexagonal courtyard—three buildings for teen boys and three for orphaned girls. Trapped like rats, the orphans stood at attention each morning.

That first morning, Officer Marjorie Shaw stood tall and dull. Her white hair was pulled into a tight, dignified bun. She unclenched her gloved hands and spoke loudly behind her mask.

"A short presentation," she said, directing the orphans' attention to a screen.

"Twelve Studios presents The Fractal City." The screen flicked a picture of the city's skyline. "Where everything is designed. Everything is art. As part of the working whole, the orphanages in the Outlands serve the great city."

"Our great Vizier, Ida Watts, crawled out of the rubble of a war-torn, intolerant land. She climbed out of a society where men denied women dignity and cruelly degraded, enslaved, physically abused, and even raped many. But Vizier Ida survived—unsilenced. She would not bow to intimidation. She no longer allowed herself to be the odd one out, the shadow, the objectified, the overlooked. The war exposed the depravity of man. Ida grew discontent with men being 'privileged' and women being 'disprivileged.' Down with the worldview that says man is good and woman is bad.

After the war ended, Ida led, designed, and built our great city from the ruins. As she rid society of narrow-mindedness, buildings and skyscrapers rose from the ashes." Contrasting images flashed onto the screen—rubble, then a beautiful city skyline.

"What will it be? Men ignited a world war. Men fought and sustained the war. It changed everything for us. The people of Eliora nearly died out because those monsters started a nuclear war. Their selfishness created the radiation that spills into our land today. Removing the radiation is our final step in rebuilding. Will you join us?

One man ruled and thought only of himself, his health, and his possessions. He hid Eliora's crystal key along with all the protective powers. He locked us in this wasteland. Now, nothing can grow. Nothing can survive outside the dome of safety we've built over the city."

"Except the Outlanders," Emma whispered to Nova, rolling her eyes. "Our tribe is so fierce that we learned to survive in this wasteland long before the Nomarchs arrived and took us to be their slaves." Nova raised an eyebrow.

"Remember when our ancestors built underground bunkers?" Try as she might, Emma couldn't let the propaganda have the last word. "It seemed like no one could kill them for a while. Then, our parents built above ground. We acclimated to this harsh environment, but the Nomarchs found us." A Nomarch flicked his gaze toward the girls. Emma closed her mouth and looked back toward the screen.

"After a challenging childhood and evil world war, a new leader arose, our Vizier—Ida Watts." A picture of a woman appeared in the film.

"She changed everything for all of us," Officer Shaw said with conviction. Marjorie's cold, fishy eyes grew as she looked at the orphans. She pointed to the screen.

"Where others tore down, Ida built. The Fractal City is now habitable because of her. Ida built a clear protective dome over the city. She established a temporary shelter in the Outlands to protect citizens from radiation poisoning. Ida built a Matriarchal society, giving a place to each overlooked woman. Everyone has a place in the working whole: the poor, disabled, and elderly." Marjorie paused, "Even Outlanders."

Shaw looked up from the podium—eyes narrowing, "Even you!" Nova rocked on her heels. A huge smile spread across Marjorie's face. "Ida Watts holds the key to unlocking peace and prosperity."

"Tolerance! Equality." Marjorie dropped a heavy fist on the podium. "Fires, storms, looting, and disasters are a thing of the past." She sighed, "And the beautiful result of Ida Watts' labor is a community where everyone stands on equal footing. Everyone works in partnership. From the grand Ensor Estate, surrounded by the sprouts of new life growing in her gardens, Ida is rebuilding our society." Shaw clicked a button on a remote, and pictures of architectural greatness, paintings, and fashionable people walking down city streets flashed onto the screen.

"Will you support Eliora from the Outlands?" was the resounding question of the presentation. "Will you build? Will you contribute? Will you give back as Eliora, our great giving mother, has given life to you?" The orphans exchanged terse nods.

A nearby chimney puffed, clouding the moon. The woodsy fragrance brought Nova back to the past. Her father sat in front of crackling logs in their first house above ground. Her mother stood at the kitchen counter, sprinkling cinnamon over a warm apple pie. She longed for her mother's roasted chicken and the holiday mugs she used to set on the counter. Each held the taste of Christmas.

Nova smiled to herself until Officer Shaw roared, "Now is the time to put our differences aside and come together and serve The Fractal City of Eliora.

You must join the larger whole to serve our great city. Only then can society work properly. Today, we honor you with your assignments." Most faces looked calm, but Nova's shoulders slumped. She stuck her hands in her pockets and swayed. She gazed at the ground, trying to steady herself.

"Ready yourselves for the training to come!" Officer Shaw stood like a stone wall. Nova glanced up. Floodlights illuminated a table at the center of the stage. It held seven frosted bowls. The left bowl had a red color, the next bowl orange, then yellow, and so on. The table ended with a violet-filled bowl.

"Now," Officer Shaw announced, "Eliora's Seer is coming to make her selections." Shaw clapped under the moonlight, "The ceremony will now begin."

Nova had never seen a Seer before and wondered if she was older than the sun—with wisdom and leathery skin to prove it. Could a Seer see straight into a person's soul? What if she could see into the spirit world? Nova's imagination ran wild. "What if the Seer has some sixth sense? And what is that paint for?"

"Iris, our very own Seer," Officer Shaw projected as she introduced a small ghostly woman." Begin your selections."

"There she is," Emma whispered. Nova stood taller. Floodlights illuminated a weatherworn woman as she hobbled across the stage. She stopped and pointed her crooked finger at the crowd. Her white winter coat looked moth-eaten and shabby.

"Those are the longest, whitest dreadlocks I've ever seen," Nova whispered. The powder-white dreds fell from the top of Iris's head to her waist. Only one purple dread hung on the left side of Iris's face.

"Astra," Officer Shaw sounded robotic. A girl with two braids walked toward the stage. "On the double now!" The child trotted faster. Iris smiled amiably. Black circle glasses nearly covered her timeworn face. Iris looked the orphan up and down with milky blue eyes magnified through her lenses. Her eyes held a hint of wildness.

"Your blessed assignment shall be River rat." Iris smacked her lips together. "You will wear protective radioactive gear and go fish along the Odalys River and work in the Outland's fish hatchery to produce white meat for the city."

Iris dipped her nobby index finger in red paint and brushed it across the orphan's forehead.

"Reds will move into bunkhouse number one," Officer Shaw ordered. A Nomarch stood ready to receive the girl, who had a look of terror hidden behind a slight smile.

"Hunter," Marjorie Shaw shouted, standing tall behind the podium. A teen boy stepped onto the stage.

"Orange," Iris said weakly. Iris's long fingernails reminded Nova of a vulture's claw. She swiped the bright color across him. "You are The Fractal City's Field rats," Iris said, limping closer to the teen. "You will build a permanent dome on the East side of Outlands to cultivate the land, garden, and harvest crops for our great city's markets."

"Bunkhouse number two," Officer Shaw pointed the teen in the right direction. Nomarchs gathered the children into their color groups in separate parts of the courtyard. The crowd of children dwindled to the last few orphans as the Seer made her selections.

"Mira," Officer Shaw projected as she read from a screen.

"You are selected to be a Roof rat," Iris spoke feebly. Colorful bangle bracelets climbed up Iris's arms and clinked as she swiped a bow of yellow paint over Mira's brow. "You will join Barrack number three. Your assignment—suit up, brave the wasteland elements, and repair the cracks in the dome." Nova's eyes shifted left toward Emma, but she was careful not to move her head.

"Cracks in the dome," Nova thought to herself as Marjorie dismissed Mira with a wave.

"Caelum." Offer Shaw's eyes scanned the remaining children. Iris hobbled forward with her wooden cane, clicking against the wooden stage. She seemed to wilt from all the exertion when she reached the bowl further down the table.

"You are assigned to be a Summit rat," Iris crowed. "You will work in the mountains, mining for precious treasures. Join the greens in barrack number four."

"Serve your city well," Officer Shaw dismissed him.

"Nova," Officer Shaw asserted. Nova saw stars—the beginnings of a migraine. Her boots sloshed through the sleet as she stepped before the Seer.

"Oh! You are in a bit of a tangle here." Iris's twinkling eyes magnified under her round black glasses. She sucked on her lips for a minute as if trying to decide what to do with her. A dark cloud covered the moon, casting a shadow over the courtyard. The air nipped—penetrating each layer of clothing. Iris wiggled her cane into a corner of the stage. She pulled at her thick coat. She stroked the faux fur. She extended her cane toward Nova's face.

"Oh...oh...yes! I'm getting something." Suddenly, the courtyard felt claustrophobic. Nova wanted to be anywhere but here, her fingers tingling at her side. Iris dipped a contorted finger in the blue paint. She marked Nova's forehead. The blue bow of paint dripped down Nova's forehead.

"Selected!" Iris mouthed. The cerulean color splashed memories onto the banks of Nova's mind: blue waves, a baby blanket, a baby's cry on the open river.

"Report to the Apothecary for further instructions. You'll stay in barrack number five."

Nova heard the Seer sort two remaining children. She assigned one boy to work as a Sewer rat in the tunnels under the city. And by the time Officer Shaw called Emma's name, Nova was rejoined by her friend. To Nova's relief, Emma had also joined the group of blues.

***

The gloomy sky choked out a dingy fog after Nova's first bone-chilling count. The cold burned Nova's nose and ears. She pulled the sleeves of her sweater to cover her red hands.

When the temperature dropped below zero, snowflakes flurried around the Apothecary. A bell chimed when a Nomarch opened the pine-green door. Two round shop windows framed the entrance, each displaying glass bottles.

"Welcome to the laboratory," said a tall Nomarch, who looked far too happy.

"Lab rats?!" Nova's eyes widened as she stepped under the Apothecary sign.

Tiny icicles hung from it. A blast from the heater warmed her face. The aromatic air smelled of cedarwood and cardamon. Nova's muddy boots carried bits of sleet into the shop. Nomarchs divided the children into different rooms.

"Go that way." The Nomarch pointed past the counter toward a secure back room. Stepping in, Nova found herself rapidly blinking. The Seer sat behind the table. Iris's extra-large eyes glinted at Nova and Emma.

"Remove your coats and enter the lab," Iris spoke feebly. Over her white lab coat, Iris pulled on an apron that seemed to weigh her down. Emma and Nova huddled together in a small tin room.

"Wait until I give you the signal." Iris's voice sounded like a crow. She looked through a little window in the door.

"Step forward." Iris's voice crackled over the intercom. A red light lit up a line across the floor. Nova shuffled forward and looked back with knitted brows. She searched Iris's face for approval.

"Step over the line," Emma and Nova took a reluctant step. The door burst open.

"Come out," Iris's fingers contorted around her cane. She hobbled forward. She waved them along, "Quickly." The girls hurried out of the room. Iris closed the door with a bang. Leaning over, she took a long breath and looked up at the girls. Emma and Nova's eyes widened in confusion.

"What do you feel?" Iris asked, eyes darting everywhere.

"I feel fine." Emma smiled awkwardly.

"What..." Nova stuttered but tried to sound brave. "What.... are we doing?" Iris's mouth formed a straight line. Magnified eyes blinked behind her circle glasses. Bangles clinked on her arm as she removed her apron.

"We are testing radiation levels." Iris croaked, clearing her throat. "Radiation levels are rising in different parts of the city. It seems to be seeping in through the cracks in the dome." Iris exhaled, "We need to know the effects." A large square table stood in the center of the Apothecary. Metal containers, paper towels, water jugs, and medical papers littered the surface. Emma's face suddenly turned ashen. Nova scratched her arms.

"I'm..." Emma whispered. "I'm not feeling well." Emma's eyes dilated. "Where is the bathroom?" Iris pointed. Emma threw a hand over her mouth as she disappeared, making walrus noises.

"My arms," Nova blurted out. "They're burning." Circles appeared. Iris snatched up her arm for a closer look.

"They're on fire." Nova shrieked. "My skin is on fire." One of the red circles boiled up. Another swelling sore broke open and oozed a clear liquid. Iris rushed over to a silver tray. Grabbing a syringe, she injected it into Nova's upper arm. "Oh," relief washed over her. "What is that?" Nova squeaked.

"Iodine." Iris rubbed the end of a medicated Q-tip across the red boils. "Better?" Big eyes stared at Nova.

"M..Hmmm," she grunted. But sparks flicked in Nova's line of vision— the beginnings of another headache. Nova massaged her temples.

"I think I...." Nova's voice trailed off as darkness overshadowed the sparks of light, and she slumped to the floor.

***

Nova lay in bed for two days. Not fully recovered, she found herself in the snow-covered Apothecary sitting outside the little tin room.

"Listen," Emma mouthed, pointing to the wall. "The Seer is saying something." Nova and Emma leaned in to eavesdrop.

"The properties of a crystal react to the radiation." The wall did not muffle the sound of the Seer's cane clacking against the floor.

"The reaction is from the electromagnetic field," Iris spoke hoarsely, "emitting an accelerated electric charge."

Nova's mind swirled. "What is this old lady even saying?"

"A solid spontaneously recovers from radiation damage." Iris stumbled with her cane. Her bangles clinked as she gripped the cane tightly.

"So, in a sense, a crystal could open up a radiation barrier?" a Nomarch interjected. Iris dragged her foot across the room like a broom: swish-swish. Nova and Emma leaned in further.

"Yes, my boy. Yes! That is why the old ruler hid Eliora's crystal key." Nova shook her head, trying to understand what the Seer was saying. Nova's head pounded at the thought of having to walk over the red line in the tin room again. She looked down at the boils on her arm and remembered the dizziness and the pounding headache.

We must find a way to contain the radiation because I believe the radiation can evolve into irreversible DNA changes. We must know all the effects," the Seer said, clutching the medallion hanging around her neck. "Lab tests showed that it targets the bloodstream, so I will call it the Red Death."

"It's a plague," Emma whispered, eyes widening. The apothecary door opened. Iris flipped a switch on the wall, making the red radiation line glow across the floor.

6

Three months passed, or had it been three years? It made no difference. Every day was the same. The horn. The call. The work. The sickness. The soup. The shallow rest. One night, sleep wouldn't come. The red bumps on Nova's arms still sent shooting pains up and down her arm. The number of people in the bunkhouse made her feel claustrophobic. The stifled air made it hard for Nova to breathe. She needed fresh air.

Without a thought, her legs slid off the side of her bunk. As quietly as she could, she moved toward the bunkhouse door. She wiggled the knob—locked. She pulled a bobby pin from her hair and slid it into the middle of the rusted keyhole. She pressed it deeper until she heard a click. Nova turned the knob and quietly stepped out.

The night air should have been fresh, but a spoiled cloud of gray smoke rose from three different chimneys, all joining together as if holding hands. The solid brick building held no windows. The sweet and spicy scent made Nova think of lilacs, garlic, horseradish, and onions. Or was it more like almonds and then a whiff of rotten eggs? Something about it was off. "Is that sulfur?" Nova asked. It wasn't right, whatever it was.

Nova walked along the barbed wire fence, avoiding patches of ice. A blustery wind whizzed by. Seeing another snow-capped barrack that held more workers and weary kids, Nova moved closer to the fenceline, feet sloshing in graying sleet. Her mind had drifted when a hooded figure appeared out of the corner of her eye.

"Wait," a cracked voice broke the silence. Nova froze, eyes wide. A skinny teen pulled back the hood of his coat.

"Nova!?" he whispered. She faced him.

"Alister? How... How are you here?" Nova gasped. Her feet stepped forward, brushing through the snow. She touched her hair when he caught eyes with her. Her best childhood friend stood before her. All separated time came together at that moment.

Nova smiled, remembering when she first met Alister at another fence line years earlier. Nova's little white dog had escaped her yard on a warmer day. Penny appeared in the neighbor's yard—like a ghost. Fluffy white fur had materialized before a floppy-eared bunny, so suddenly, it's a wonder the poor rabbit didn't faint on the spot. If the bunny's nerves weren't already shot, Penny, the playful pup, started popping around the yard like popcorn. The bunny didn't know which way to run, so it stared wide-eyed. Alister had heard the yipping dog from his yard, so he jumped the fence to rescue the poor bunny from the wired-haired terrier with a dime-store nose. Just as he had grabbed the dog, Nova had come running. Her eyes darted around, and she swallowed hard as she reached the close-board fenceline.

"It's ok," a voice said on the other side of the fence. "She didn't hurt the bunny." The sun peaked out from behind a gray cloud.

"Oh good." Nova blushed and compulsively scratched her nose. "She is so wild."

"Here." The little dog's white, fluffy face appeared above the fence. Nova scooped Penny into her arms.

"You naughty little thing!" She began her motherly rebuke. Nova put the little dog in the house and returned to find the boy in her yard.

"This is where she got out. Let me help you fill this hole." That memory was the first of many. Seeing Alister at a fenceline again made Nova smile like it was Christmas morning. All distant spaces met at this exact point. As if every moment before caved into a speck, the longing for friendship now met in time and space. Smiles exploded on their faces like the light of a shooting star. The universe brightened.

"I've missed you," Alister grinned. He tilted his head to lean in. The faint hum of the electrical fence built a barrier between the two.

"I can't believe this," Nova's smile widened. Her arms opened before her. "I can't believe you are here. I could hug you!"

"Are you ok?" Alister asked.

"I'm ok," Nova gulped. A longing to tell him everything rose up. "My family..." A dog's bark echoed through the night air.

"The guards." Alister's deep brown eyes flicked toward the brick bunkhouse.

"Quick, take this." A small loaf of bread flew through a small square opening on the fence. The bread fell into a pile of snow. Nova's knees hit the ground as she dove to rescue it.

"Go! Nova. They're coming."

7

The next night, it happened so suddenly; it was unlike anything before. Nova gasped in her bed. Emma clapped a pale hand over Nova's mouth.

"Shhh..." She hissed, holding a finger to her lips with her free hand. "If you keep making noise, they'll hear." Nova went quiet. "Better... Now listen. Go to the fenceline in two minutes. Alister asked for you." The wind whistled in the window. A crooked shutter creaked outside. Without a word, Nova climbed out of her bunk and reached for her bobby pin. Paint peeled off the wall. She took her jacket from the foot of her bed and slipped her arm through the hole. Floorboards creaked as she stepped toward the door. She carefully avoided the pulled-up floor panels.

Under a dark sky, Nova pulled her coat tightly around herself as she left behind the musky house. The icy wind blew over the snow-covered land. Snow crunched and crackled under her feet. Nova faced the humming fence. Brown eyes under a mop of curly hair stared back at her. A shaky hand pulled out a letter. The crinkled paper slid through the barbed wire.

"Hide it," the boy said with a huff of breath. He walked away as quickly as he'd come. The wind surrounded him, screeching like an owl.

***

Nova opened the letter in the dim light of the bunkhouse. Alister had pulled black ink into lines of cursive. Initially stunned by the fact that Alister's writing didn't look like chicken scratch, Nova smiled. His writing was, in fact, quite neat:

I've missed you. Her heart warmed at his words. *I miss laughing with you. Everything seems so busy, noisy, dark, and confusing. And yet, it's still somehow been so quiet without you around. Each day, I want to tell you about the things we've fixed or the time we got lost in the underground sewer system for two hours. It was wild.*

But I mainly want to write to tell you a story. As far back as our people go, there was a time before us— a time of a ruler called the Sovereign.

"Does he mean the Vizier?" Nova questioned, adjusting her pillow. As if the letter read her mind, it answered, *Now, the Sovereign is someone different than the Vizier.* Nova's forehead wrinkled. *I know you've heard your entire life that the Vizier is the designer of Eliora and all the building projects are her legacy, but listen to the story. There once was a different ruler, a good ruler before the violent man and deceptive woman who'd led in the last few years.* A guard's shadow passed over the door. Black boots scuffed to a stop. Nova stuffed the letter under her blanket and pretended to be asleep.

***

"I think he likes you," Emma teased, waving the letter before Nova.

"Emma! Give that back." Nova jumped on her friend to wrestle the letter out of her hand.

"Ok. Ok." Emma gasped, pressed between the bedsheets and her friend. She sucked in a strangled breath. "You're right. We can't know that *for sure.*" Emma rolled her eyes at Nova, who finally retrieved the letter. "He only wants to meet up and talk all the time. He wants to tell you *all* about his day. What guy wants to talk about his day, *Nova*?!" Emma's eyes grew wide. Nova's cheeks flushed.

"You know what you're suggesting isn't even legal," Nova whispered loudly and good-naturedly nudged her with an elbow. Emma's funny face smiled mischievously.

***

"You look nice today," Alister said, eyes lighting up when he saw her.

Nova's face flushed. She looked at her feet but smiled. Nova only spurred Alister to make silly faces that made her laugh out loud.

"Did your mom ever read you that book, *Barbapapa*?"

"Barb-A-Papa," Nova's voice lowered three octaves. She crossed her eyes as she whisper-sang utter nonsense, showing her true self.

"Bar-ba Mama," Alister added to make it a duet. A genuine laugh burst out. Nova clapped a hand over her mouth. When guards didn't patrol as quickly as expected, the two momentarily broke from their sad reality into a fit of hysterics.

"No, but I've heard you talk about it so much that I feel like I could read it to you." Nova snorted, which made her laugh until her sides hurt. "I mean, I feel like I know it because I can sing the *theme* song." Both of their shoulders bobbed so vigorously that it was only a matter of time before sniggering would erupt into full-blown laughter. Without even saying goodbye, they both made a run for their barracks.

***

Weeks later, Nova found another moment to sneak out. She avoided the snow drifts on the bunkhouse steps. Clouds covered the moon, making the fence line darker than usual. It hid the fact that Nova wasn't the only one who snuck out of the bunkhouse.

"Do you have enough food?" Alister tilted his head.

"I'm okay," Nova shrugged her shoulders. "They added oatmeal for breakfast."

"I was able to get an extra sweater. Here—I know it gets cold in the bunkhouse," Alister felt the wind's chill as he passed the cardigan through the sharply barbed fence.

"Thank you," whispered Nova, holding it close to her chest. "How's the underground?"

"I got to work under the city again this week. We were working on a drain pipe under the Ensor Gardens."

"Gardens—like actual living plants? Could you see them?" Nova grinned until she saw squinting eyes peek out from behind the side of the bunkhouse.

"Emma." Nova thought, lips tightening. Emma's ear appeared to grow as she sidestepped closer to the fence line to listen. Nova's eyes narrowed. She screamed in her mind,

"Go. Home!" But upon seeing Alister again, a giant smile grew across her face, and she acted like everything was normal.

"Yeah!" Alister said. "It was so green. I saw part of it through the grate. Right above me, there was a flower clock. Lilies and roses grow there. The groundskeeper, a lady named Gwyn, told me that each flower blooms at a different hour. It's like magic."

"I'll have to tell Emma." Nova smiled. Nova gave Emma the go-home-right-now-or-I'll- come-over-there stare. Emma fluttered her eyes. Nova cocked her head to the side and tried to ignore her friend's batting eyelashes. She redirected her attention to Alister. "But how can it survive in this frozen wasteland? Especially with the radiation?"

"I know, right?!" Alister said. "It's so weird. It's like the flowers drink in the radiation or something. Get this: Gywn has been losing her eyesight from radiation exposure, but she said she can see when she enters the garden." A flurry whistled through the barbed fence. "I'm sure the dome helps, but to think, in the middle of the wilderness, there is a beautiful garden. Emma ducked back into the bunkhouse with a guilty grin.

"Haven't you heard the Outlander's song?" Alister took a deep breath and closed his eyes. Soon, his baritone voice sounded out softly:

All will bloom in the Hour of the Lily
in the garden center.
A star's spark will light the throne
of the rightful heir.
A leaf will fall,
but roots go down deep.
The gift is the key
that will open the door.
Look for a son among the people.
Ask him to set his people free.

Nova paused, soaking in the song's meaning and the fact that Alister could actually sing.

"Oh! and there is this tree. I've never seen anything like it in my life. The leaves seem alive somehow." The snow crunched under Alister's boots as he stood taller and talked faster." They look like lava or fire or something."

"It's hard to imagine since everything is so snowy out here. Why doesn't everybody notice or talk about how amazing that is?" Nova asked.

"Everything is so dehumanized no one notices beauty anymore."

"You'll have to sneak me down there someday." Nova mirrored Alister's excitement and laughed at her ridiculousness.

"I'll find a way," Alister winked. "But be warned, if you see it, you'll want to paint it." Alister remembered the time he climbed into Nova's treehouse and found her surrounded by red and blue paint, messy brushes, and art pinned to every wall.

"It's been so long since I've held a brush," Nova smiled with closed lips. "What I wouldn't give for a canvas and a brush."

"Well, one day, I'll find a way to get you down there, and you can paint it," Alister said, smiling mischievously.

"And I suppose you, sir, have a map of the entire underground memorized?"

"How did you know?!" Alister asked, eyes squinted. "It is a fascinating layout." Alister went on, "I'm curious who designed it. It works like underground streets."

"You could get anywhere really–oh–did you read my letter?" Alister interrupted himself.

"Yes, and I have one question about it," Nova whispered. "If there is a Sovereign—where is he?" Nova slouched,

"People in the city live in mansions, and we are out here suffering?" She shoved her hands into her pockets. "Why is evil winning?"

"They don't see it that way. They think they're making things better."

"I know. I'm sorry. I should believe you; it feels like we'll be stuck here forever." Alister moved closer to the humming fence,

"He will come, Nova," Alister smiled. "And then we can be together. No fences."

"But how?" White wind blasted around them, hissing.

"Remember the song," Alister said.

"So we are looking for someone's son?" Nova asked, rubbing the tips of her fingers together. "You are one of the last boys alive." Her head hurt. "There aren't any other people. No one is allowed to have a boy, let alone keep him."

"It doesn't have to stay that way." Alister stepped closer, looking deep into her eyes. She looked down at her shoes. The Nomarch's words circled in her mind, "Is marriage worth it?"

"Just imagine life and freedom in the city with the rightful ruler." Alister whispered close to Nova's ear, "We could be together."

"My father used to say that to my mother." Nova rubbed her temples. "He said they would always be together. He should be here." Nova looked up, and half closed her eyes.

"I know you are scared. I am, too, but can I tell you a secret?" Nova's eyebrows arched at Alister's question. "I love you," he whispered in the dark. "I always have—from the minute I saw you at the backyard fence."

"Alister," Nova cautioned. "You are so important to me, and that is such a big commitment. Are you sure you want to say that to me right now?"

Alister looked at Nova, pupils dilating. His heart rate accelerated. "I love you. I'm sure. I'm not asking you to say anything right now, but promise me you'll think about it."

"Ok." Nova self-consciously crossed her arms over her chest and looked through the humming fence.

***

"That is basically a marriage proposal!" Emma squealed. "He told you he loved you, which is asking you to think about running away with him. How is that not a marriage proposal?!"

Nova sat on the edge of the bunk bed. Butterflies took flight in her stomach. Excitement danced around anxiety. Questions swirled, "I know he's gone out of his way to help me, even if it was a small thing—a sweater, soup, medicine, a good book— but is this the right time to decide something this big? How can I possibly let him risk this?" Nova enjoyed Alister's companionship, but a heavy dread and a twinge of panic rose when she faced commitment. It wasn't that she didn't trust him. She did wholeheartedly. He had proved his character. She had a deep affection and love for him. She just couldn't bear the thought of losing someone else.

"Everyone I have ever loved is gone. I can't lose him too," Nova whispered. "How could it even work?" Nova paused, slowing down to breathe deeply.

"You can be together," Emma said. "He knows the underground. He will do everything in his power to protect you."

"I know," Nova smiled gently. "But it's so risky."

"Think about it, though," Emma looked her in the eye. "They've already taken everything else. Are you going to let them take this too? If you self-preserve, you'll still end up alone."

"True." Nova's mind whirled as she lay awake late into the night.

***

"But how could we get married if I can't even cook?" Nova's eyes sparkled. Alister nearly spewed the water he was drinking.

"Because that's the worst of our problems?" returned Alister with a smirk.

"Just imagine the multi-tasking that would take. How am I supposed to stir the meat, peel the potatoes, and drain the peas all at the same time?"

"Stop. You are making me hungry," Alister held his stomach. "Do you remember when we had meals like that— the ones your mom used to make? Oh, what I would give for a real meal right now."

"And a warm fire," Nova added. "Alister, my mom didn't teach me to do measurements." Alister's brow arched. "I don't even know how to turn a stick of butter into half of a cup of butter." Alister bit his lip.

"It's a stick!" Nova blurted out. Her arms dropped by her side.

"Shhhh. They'll hear," Alister held a finger to his lips and pointed to the guard tower.

"What if I wanted to make you a cake on our anniversary," Nova whispered loudly. "And I chose upside-down pineapple cake?"

"I like that kind of cake," Alister shrugged. "That would be fine."

"The oven would probably swallow the cake batter and spit out charcoal. Just imagine it; I'd have to debut the cake representing my love for you," Nova clutched her heart. "As upside down chocolate cake. Not right side up burnt cake." Nova pinned her chin to her shoulder dramatically.

"I love you, Nova Bromley," Alister laughed.

***

Alister and Nova took the risk of seeing each other as often as possible. Small pieces of sharp, pointed wire twisted around the humming electric fence. The cold air couldn't be contained. The wind blew and swept up Nova's golden hair. Stars lit the winter sky like snowflakes, ready to fall. Snow-capped guard towers stood at each corner of the courtyard and at the fenceline behind each bunkhouse.

"I saw the city too, not just the gardens," Alister said.

"Wait?! How?" Nova's arms dropped to her side.

"A few weeks ago, our crew was working in the drain pipes, and I saw the streets and tall buildings." Alister grinned sideways. "The buildings are huge."

"You know some people spend their whole lives in the Outlands, right?" Nova tucked her hair behind her ear.

"But listen..." Alister interrupted. "We need to get to the underground below the city."

"Why?" Nova questioned.

"I heard someone talking about radiation barriers or leaks." Alister faced her.

"A radiation barrier?" Nova hugged her arms around herself, standing in the gusty wind.

"I heard the worker say that the Nomarchs are building barriers to keep people in certain parts of the city."

Nova's mouth opened. Stuttering, she said, "Wait...but... Tha... That's not what the Seer said. She said they were trying to contain the radiation. Are you sure?"

"I saw them building it," Alister's shrugged. "I watched from the drainpipe, and I heard them talking."

"Alister, do you know what happens if you cross the barrier?"

He shook his head.

"You get sick. It starts like a normal sickness, and then it gets wild." Her voice lowered to almost a whisper, "The Seer is calling it the Red Death." Nova lifted her sleeve and revealed red boils. The moment Alister saw Nova's injury, something rose inside of him. A tidal wave of affection crashed in and flooded his heart.

"I love her." The thought solidified. It was the most dangerous feeling he had ever felt. He tried to suppress the emotion but couldn't. Alister gazed intensely, deeply, and passionately into Nova's deep brown eyes. He leaned closer to the fence and whispered, "I'll do everything I can to protect you."

***

The next night's conversation led to another. Days turned into weeks. Months became years. Nova snuck out of the barracks every chance she got to meet the boy at the fenceline. Most conversations lasted mere minutes because of the Nomarch's night patrols, but over ten years— sneaking looks and sharing books, they came to know almost everything there was to know about each other. Alister shared the books he read at night, from arithmetic to history and art. He had an eye for design. And what he taught had the same clarity and structure.

One day, Nova noticed how thick Alister's neck had become. His shoulders broadened. Nova herself reached a new height. A teenage boy and young lady no longer stood at the fence, but a man and woman stood facing each other.

Alister's face shone like the sun by day. Nova stood under the same sky, reflecting a smile like the moon at night. How miraculous and balanced the man and woman seemed together.

***

"Get up!" Nova whispered. "I'm serious. Get up."

"I have to get down on one knee, Nova," Alister laughed.

"What if they see you?" Nova's eyes frantically darted along the fenceline for any movement.

"I love you. I want to spend the rest of my life with you. You are so beautiful, and I want you to be my wife. Will you marry me?" A silly smirk grew on Nova's face. "Will you eat the meals I make?"

"Every day," Alister gave her a wide-eyed look. Nova stepped closer to the fence. Determination rose inside her. She knew the risks firsthand but promised, "Tomorrow then."

"Tomorrow. We'll meet at the Glistening Tree in the Ensor Gardens."

8

Mud-stained heaps leaned against the barracks, each snow pile littering the courtyard. Nova shivered. She clenched her jaw tighter to keep her teeth from chattering. Nomarchs opened the fences to the adjoining bunkhouses, and everyone filed in like on the day Nova had arrived. Oblivious to everyone except one young man, she looked straight ahead, trying not to gaze at him for too long. But no matter where Nova looked, she always knew where Alister was. She tried to focus her attention on the stage, but like the shining sun, she felt Alister's presence without directly looking at him. His presence made her feel warm inside; she was drawn to him.

More people arrived in the courtyard for count. Space got tighter. Officer Shaw stood behind a podium with a row of Nomarchs lined up at attention. Gray clouds moved to cover the sky. Marjorie Shaw's words filled the hexagonal courtyard.

"Attention!" Nova's head pounded as the siren screamed. "Hear The Edict of Eliora: Most honored daughters of Eliora, today our glorious leader, Ida Watts, has put forth a new mandate. We will locate the daughters from every territorial division." Marjorie Shaw's voice grew louder. "Each orphaned girl aged twelve through twenty-five and every future daughter born in Amity under The Tolerance Law shall gather in the city gate–entrance number six to fulfill her royal calling in walking relationships. The matriarchal harem on the east side of the Ensor Estate will welcome girls from every nome who are found worthy." The siren sounded again, and red lights flashed outside the bunkhouses.

"Ladies, please proceed to the city gate." Officer Shaw released the girls and young women from count. Overhead, dark storm clouds rolled in, but the lightning bolt moment struck Nova when Officer Shaw hissed,

"Go."

Nova didn't speak or whisper, but Alister and Nova made eye contact. That was when Nova could taste it—fear. Like tissues pulled out of a tissue box, Nomarchs plucked girls out of count.

"Go. Go. Go!" a Nomarch with a red cuff band on his left arm, black boots, and a peaked cap thundered. He waved his arm. His words broke Nova's trance. A loud sound cracked, then snapped. Shoved by a Nomarch, Nova slid on a patch of ice. She released a bone-chilling scream that ignited everyone into action.

Short, tall, young, and older girls pushed forward. A singular, irrational mentality took over when they heard the high-pitched sound. Confusion pushed. Chaos shoved.

"Nova lay on the frozen ground amid the stampede. A wave of girls crashed and slid over her. A boot crushed her hand. Another teen tripped over her. The great hope to escape further abuse from the Nomarchs burned so fiercely that one girl accidentally stepped on Nova's face.

"Nova!" Emma raced forward, trampling over the white blanket of snow that covered the sleeping earth.

"Uhh..." Nova's long blonde hair covered her face as she groaned.

"Come on," Emma grabbed Nova's arm and pulled her up. "Are you alright?" Nova wiped the blood from her lip and nodded despite the tears in her eyes. Another girl bumped into them. Emma's dark eyes squinted as she pressed her lips together.

"Stay with me," Emma grabbed Nova's hand and led her forward. "Don't let go."

Fear continued to spread in many of the young girls. Panic spread like wildfire as the Nomarchs herded the girls like cattle toward a semi-truck. With each step, Nova's heart thumped so loudly that the shouting Nomarchs seemed muted. Her hands trembled.

"Get in." A Nomarch pushed Nova with the back of his gun. The jolt played a memory in her mind like a movie. She rewatched Marjorie Shaw scream, "Get back" to her father. She was back on the dock with her family.

He had just wanted to protect her brother. Nova closed her eyes and tried to take a deep breath, but each inhale was shallow and sharp. The wind howled around her winter footsteps. The arctic blast peeled back a layer, revealing the landscape's bare structure. Here she was again, in a different location, but the Nomarchs before her had the same type of guns, ugly gas masks, and mouths full of curses to move.

"This can't be the whole story," Nova's cerebral merry-go-round spun with agitation, confusion, and self-torturing memories.

"Watch your step," Emma pointed at the bar on the back of the truck. Nova climbed in next to Emma. The trailer offered no ventilation. The door closed, and the engine rumbled as the truck laboriously hauled itself away from the gate. There were no lavatories and only one small hole of light on the side of the trailer. "Has someone taken a screwdriver to that?" Nova asked herself.

Minutes into the trip, Nova summoned her courage and peeked through the eyeglass hole to see the Outlands. The red sky stretched across the horizon of fields that stood next to her childhood home. She could almost see behind the lion's head door-knocker. An oak table dared guests to bring all their undeserving fingerprints. The half-eaten fruit resting on the table mocked her. How often had she and Alister sat at that table together after playing? Nova remembered her mom handing them snacks and saying, "Go outside." The river at the bottom of the hill slowly disappeared as Nova left the Outlands.

All too soon, clouds billowed. Rain hammered and splattered drops against the side of the truck. Nova sat gazing into the distance. Emma shivered in the frigid air as minutes turned into hours. At points, Nova struggled not to collapse against the weight of crushing bodies. A brown-haired teen pressed up against Nova and heaved forcefully. The lingering odor caused her stomach to turn. Emma's pale and expressionless face swayed as the trailer bumped and rattled.

Worse than all the filth was Nova's desire for water. Her throat burned. Her blue, swollen lips craved a single drop. She imagined how it would trace its way inside her mouth. Dark circles formed under her deep-brown eyes as thirst tormented her—robbing her of all sleep. Nova crossed her arms, holding her elbows. For thirty-six hours, the truck carried her deeper and deeper into the land she feared— away from the man she loved.

At last, pulling into the station, the wheels screeched. After the truck stopped completely, the Nomarchs unbarred the back doors. Like infants, the women and teens crawled through the opening on their hands and knees. Nova's legs shook beneath her as the other girls poured out of the trailer. A brown-haired teen slumped over, unconscious. Nova breathed heavily.

"Are you ok? Nova began to shake her, "Wake up." The girl's eyes wouldn't open.

"Leave her," a Nomarch barked. Trembling, Nova slowly lowered herself out of the trailer. A sea of pallid girls dotted the truck stop. Just beyond the sidewalk, Nova spotted a mound of snow.

Crawling forward, She raised white pieces of ice toward her cracked lips. She devoured it like an animal.

***

"The city gates," Emma pointed. Ahead stood two gray limestone walls. Their open arms ushered Nova, Emma, and the truckload of other girls into the city's hold. White pearl-topped poles unfastened its iron doors at the V-shaped point, opening into a small archway. A sign above the entryway read, "The Eye of the Needle."

Nova entered a large vaulted room inside the city walls at the sixth entrance. Six rooms attached themselves to the main chamber, three on either side of the hexagonal atrium. This place was no ordinary gate but a small world of business.

Looking around the skylit central court, Nova could guess from the three hundred other confused faces that no one had ever seen the city.

"What are we supposed to do now?" Nova chewed on her lip.

"I don't know," Emma crossed her arms. "I guess just sit here like the others." The girls took a seat among the other girls. Nova locked one ankle behind the other and wondered what Alister was doing right then. In Nova's twenty-one years of life, with all her experience, she could only gasp like a simpleton, "Me? Us? What for? Why did this have to happen now? She repeated the question to herself a million times but had yet to hear an answer. "Right when we had made our plan and knew this was the right time." The journey of another separation felt like a somersault from the familiar into an unknown state. Nova had been one night away from having a family again. She'd been one night away from his whispers in her ear and being held in his arms. The earthquake of displacement shook her to the core. She wiped her clammy hands over her legs as the flickerings of a migraine started again.

   Yes, Nova had seen pictures of the city, but never once did she stop to consider what life as a citizen would be like —without the one she loved. Yet the city gates swung wide open, and she entered like a bleating sheep, repeating, "Me? Why?" She picked her cuticles, "They took my whole family. And now they are taking me away from Alister. Who can go untouched? What will remain unshattered?" The ache solidified her longing. She would marry. She would do whatever it would take. "They will not take everything from me," she spoke shakily. Emma heard her mumbling and squeezed her hand as if she knew that when Nova entered the city gates, the door to her past life would be closed firmly behind her. The deadbolt locked it away–shut once and for all.

"We'll find him," Emma held her gaze —daring to hope. "I will help you get to him. I know he'll come for you."

   A delicate, six-pointed star crowned the summit of the vaulted room and shone self-luminous. Nova craned her neck to look at the incredible light. It was an exquisite timber lantern. Officer Shaw stepped onto the stage and motioned for all the girls to be silent. Her voice boomed from the podium,

"Welcome, most honored Ladies of Eliora."

9

Red Room #1

"Number?" A Nomarch asked at the first checkpoint in the red-walled room of the city gates. Her shoulders drooped, "022687."

"Birthdate?" He inquired as he scribbled her name in cursive.

"August 22." He made no eye contact.

Nova bit her lip. The Nomarch traced her age, twenty-one, into the ledger and stood up. With shallow eyes and a stiff face, the Nomarch motioned her forward with his left arm.

"Put this gas mask on and cross the radiation barrier. Then go through security." She felt pain as a Nomarch inserted a needle into her arm.

"Iodine," he said.

Orange Room #2

Nova had nothing except what was in her jacket pockets. Riffling through them, she pulled out a small rag, coins, and crinkled papers. Emma did the same. A stout, attentive Nomarch reached for their documents. Nova's feet shuffled forward under the ever-watching camera. In the orange-walled room, a series of scans and searches began. Oh, how she wished to be back in the security of Alister's presence.

Yellow Room #3

Reaching the hexagonal atrium again, Nova noticed an opening into a third room labeled decontamination. Emma pointed to the sign with radiograph eyes. It hung above a set of moving doors that seemed under their own authority.

"Go through." A Nomarch waved them through. Nova followed Emma until the girls paused in a light yellow room. Decontamination was smaller than she expected. The small box of a room led to two channels that opened. Five girls disappeared to the left. Nova and Emma stepped right.

They started their journey through the labyrinth. Rounding the second corner, Nova heard a voice echo down the corridor. Waves of sound carried the voice, splashing it against every wall. A haunting discord of voices immersed the hall in a symphony of high-pitched screams. Tiny hairs stood up on Nova's arms.

Water splashed, and the sound of a whip cracked wh-tch. Her chest tightened. Emma grabbed Nova's arm and waited until the corridor's mouth closed mute. One step forward. Two. Three. Nova's heartbeat matched the irregular pattern of her feet. Like a lab rat, she turned two more corners in the maze.

Two Nomarchs instructed the girls to descend into a narrow lane of clear water. Nova and Emma passed under a white sign with black engraved letters that read: $SightH_2O$.

"Sight water." As they approached the coruscating sea of tiny polished stars, she whispered to Emma. She was interrupted by a Nomarch's mechanical voice. He sat perched atop his stool. He couldn't have been older than sixteen. He leaned against a podium, speaking into a crackling microphone, "The purifying water suspends particles, parasites, bacteria—any virus you may carry. It removes undesirable chemicals and biological contaminants and suspends unwanted solids and gases. Public health is our goal. Please remove your shoes and proceed through $SightH_2O$."

Nova slipped off her boots and approached the glistening pool. Emma lifted her hands above the water, following closely behind. Nova pulled her jacket close to her chest and waded into the glimmering water. A soft blue light marked each footprint. The water came up to her ankles. On her right, a Nomarch measured the liquid from the side of the pool. He pushed his silver rod into the $SightH_2O$. The water squirmed, lighting up—glowing like a jellyfish. It sparked like lightning in the deep night sky. Then, just as quickly as the light appeared, it disappeared. Eyes wide, Nova descended. The water slid around her softly, each ripple shining light. Her skin brightened. It transformed. It felt smooth and fresh.

Again, the Nomarch's tool plumbed the depths, bringing a second flash through the water. By that time, the water reached Nova's waist. Soon, she could no longer touch the bottom. She swam forward.

Emma kicked her feet behind her. Glimpses of childish joy raced through the girls with every stroke. Turning her head, Nova found relief with each new breath. She left a trail of blue embers—a line of cerulean sparks, a lustrous sea of stars. At the end of the water lane, Nova ascended three steps. A Nomarch motioned her and Emma into a black room, joining five other girls. Each girl hugged herself, teeth chattering. The doors closed, and a solid darkness enclosed the space. Water bubbled up, plopping at their feet. Beads of water threaded along the lines of the lit floor until each one splashed apart, flooding the ground. Windows in the roof opened up, showering rain on the women. It was a simple filtration system, but no unwanted particles could pass through the lattice-structured floor.

Nova stood sopping wet. Water dripped off the end of her nose and the edges of her blonde hair. The intercom preached, "Please remain still as our short-wave ultraviolet lights are about to come on. We use these lights for your safety. It will inactivate harmful microorganisms, destroy nucleic acids, and expose all corrupted DNA. Eliara is inhospitable to all deadly bacteria, viruses, molds, and other pathogens. Please remain still for your safety."

A purple hue overshadowed the ebony-dressed girls as the black lights flipped on. Waves of violet eclipsed the room. Nova's eyes struggled to grow accustomed to the room. Squinting, she searched for Emma.

All the girls stood motionless, cold hands hanging by their sides until a Nomarch removed a girl. The darkness grew in her absence, swelling in the stillness. She left no trace, no name, no face, no legacy. Nova's muscles tightened. "Wha...Where are they taking her?"

She caught eyes with Emma just ahead of her. She noted Emma's brown bob, the wet bangs that framed her dark eyes, and how her mouth formed a straight line. A dark fog surrounded the girl next to Emma, and a Nomarch removed that girl too. The darkness closed her eyes, reaching its hand over her mouth—silencing her. The shadow grew—overtaking the girl. She blended into it until she disappeared completely.

Nomarchs took the girls away individually, uniting them with the dark fog. The black flood blotted out all five girls. Barely breathing, Nova stood next to Emma, hands trembling. Face down, Nova saw a white speck at the center of her dress—the dot generated light. Nova's chest warmed with a tingling sensation. She marveled at it. The light brought that breathtaking feeling when standing on the edge of a Grand Canyon. The wind blows gently, and you can only slow down and breathe it in.

Each lustrous dust-sized light multiplied and gleamed. Each small light sparkled like a diamond against a black velvet backdrop. Nova's petite structure formed a glass prism, shining forth tiny fractals of light until a full range of colors illuminated her dress. Like a stained-glass window, the light seemed to pass through her. She glanced at Emma. The light was on her too.

Without warning, sirens screeched. Red lights in every corner of the room flashed. Nova stumbled back two steps. A computerized voice erupted, "Contaminated. Contaminated."

Green Room #4

"Go to room four." The Nomarch pointed. There was no trial, jury, or defense, only an elderly judge clutching his power weapon. Nova and Emma presented themselves to the magistrate, perched behind a cherry-wood desk at the peak of the triangular green walled room. He looked down at Nova over his long, curved nose. His black bug-like eyes squinted under his white wig until a scoffing smile zipped across his face. Without a hearing, the gavel fell. Judgment bound them. Condemnation vibrated off the courtroom walls: "You have crossed over radiation barriers unprotected, which has contaminated your DNA beyond repair."

Nova's mind whirled as she thought about the little tin room with a glowing red line. She could hear the Seer's voice like it was yesterday, "Step over the line." It all came flooding back—the sparks that flicked in her line of vision and the darkness that overshadowed everything.

"You guys wanted me to walk over the line," she thought, raising her eyebrows. Her mind shot off rapid-fire questions, "Are you going to take me back to the Apothecary?" Her eyes narrowed as she frowned. "What does it even mean to be contaminated beyond repair?"

The judge leaned forward, "As contaminated Outlanders, you will not be allowed entrance into the harem or walking relationships. He kept steady eye contact, "However, you are permitted to take the aptitude test to serve on a small design team. If you pass, you'll have restricted access to your work area. If you don't pass, we'll return you to the Outlands."

Blue room #5

Dragging Nova into a sterile, blue-walled room, the Nomarchs separated her from Emma. The room overlooked a spotless floor with medical beds. They lined the long triangle room.

IV drip lines with bags of fluid hung beside each bed. Nomarchs stood stiff at attention as a justice guard held out Nova's papers. A dark-eyed Nomarch glanced down at the judge's two-word verdict.

"Lie on the table." Three Nomarchs restrained Nova's shoulders and legs with thick belts.

"Please, no..." A forceful hand squeezed her arm. Nova's knuckles whitened, her lips pinched together–face flushing.

"Sit still." The Nomarch's hot breath surrounded her face. Nova closed her eyes and clung to her memory of Alister at the fenceline: his friendship, gifts of bread, and kind words. "I will not sacrifice a lifetime of love in the terror of this moment."

Minutes slowed—unraveling, unwrapping, and undoing. A rough finger trailed over her arm as if searching for something. Nova's face twisted into a painful grimace.

"Outlander," the Nomarch grinned. "The SightH_2O never lies. Because the judge found some part of you to be contaminated beyond cleansing, you will be contained to certain parts of the city." A petite white-dressed nurse hurried over with a silver tray. It held a red-tipped rod. Nova had not prepared herself for what came next.

As the doctor came closer, her pulse quickened. The nurse smiled at the Nomarch as he spoke.

"Repeat after me." The doctor said, "Please brand me, Master. Do me this one honor." Nova's heart pounded in her ears. Did she whisper the words? The Nomarch gripped the cauterizing device. A charcoal-like smell arose. The procedure took about ten minutes. Nomarchs muffled her screams as the smell of burning tissue saturated the room. Each hot line eroded a two-inch star-shaped brand on her left wrist. The ornamental pattern had six points. The symbol, the scar, the sign, marked her permanently. It was the Nomarch's last memory with Nova, the marked girl.

10

Officer Shaw isolated contaminated Outlanders into a separate room within the city gates.

"Take a seat," she ordered. "We will begin the preparation of the arts test." There were no study notes or professors to consult. Emma sat several rows behind Nova, who dared not look back. Emma's presence brought some relief.

"Miss Hart," Marjorie Shaw said as a female Nomarch stepped into the classroom.

"My name is Olivia Hart, and I will be proctoring today's test." Her red-tinted curls parted in the middle of her head and formed a triangle. "Before we take the test, we will watch a short film."

Her pale arms highlighted the screen. "This is *Envision*." Nova had just noticed the TV.

"Focus," Nova scolded herself. She needed to be less focused on Miss Hart's bright green uniform. The Peter Pan collar highlighted her natural beauty. And her tight elbow-length sleeves revealed how thin she was. The bright colors reminded Nova of a crayon box.

"Red, green, blue, and yellow," Nova thought as she counted the stripes on her sleeves. Repeat. "I can't remember the last time I saw this much color." Miss Hart flipped the lights on after a presentation video.

"*Envision* has three parts. The written exam, the preparation of the art portion, and the aptitude test. Let's begin."

**

Nova turned in her written exam at the front desk as the Nomarch had instructed.

"In the preparation of the arts portion," the teacher added, "you will be quizzed on color theory. You will do an analysis on artwork and a three-page drawing exam." Nova quickly found herself back at the front desk, turning in the second portion of the test.

"We will move on to the aptitude test to determine your skills and propensity to succeed in various activities," Miss Hart announced. "We will assess how you will likely perform in an area without prior training. This is not about knowledge or intelligence but about your tendency toward various strengths and weaknesses." Miss Hart cleared her throat, "This test will measure your competency in logic, numerical skills, verbal abilities, as well as critical thinking and problem-solving abilities."

The test was unlike any Nova had taken. No pencil. No paper. No lightning bolt designs of gray-filled dots like the standardized tests her Mom made her take. In a small room, she sat alone in a medical chair—a monitoring band wrapped around Nova's head. Rubber gloves brushed against her forehead, setting it. Other girls averted their eyes as they passed the open door to take their tests in adjoining rooms.

"This will take three minutes." Keres, a female Nomarch with thin, gold-rimmed glasses, fastened it tighter. Nova stared at a white clinical wall with two black and white photos. The band compressed. The pressure squeezed Nova's forehead tightly.

Nova felt the vinyl recliner covered in plastic stick to the back of her legs. The minutes marched by. One. Two. Three. High heels clicked down the corridor.

"Stand up." Beads clinked around the Nomarch's neck. Dizzy, Nova complied. The computer spat out a piece of paper. Snatching it, the Nomarch read it.

"Your results are in." Green eyes widened. "Clear results. Hmmm. It's your lucky day." Nova slid her legs off the side of the chair and stood. The Nomarch pointed at the papers, "As you know, Contaminated Outlanders with corrupted DNA are not permitted to work in the harem."

"Ok," Nova spoke meekly. She pressed her lips together to hide her relief. "I'm so glad I'm not going to the harem," she thought.

"You showed aptitude in art," the Nomarch handed her a pamphlet. "So you will not be returned to the Outlands." Nova's heart sank at the thought of Alister back in the Outlands. "You will remain in the city to work on a design team in the Legacy Hall." Another paper found its way into Nova's hand.

"Will I ever see Emma again?" Nova glanced down at the documents.

"You will be moved to an isolated west wall flat instead of a matriarchal home, and you'll have restricted access to parts of the city due to radiation barriers. But you'll have access to your workstation in the Legacy Hall as an *Ideogram Artist.*"

Keres held out the rest of the papers. "From now on, you will preserve the legacy of Ida Watts. You'll need to get supplies: paintbrushes, papyrus, books, and paint. Here are those printed orders. You'll be transported to your flat in the west wall tonight and find everything on Oort Street tomorrow morning." Before Nova could finger through the papers, Nomarchs ushered her out of the room to her new home.

II

The City

11

The Legacy Hall spanned the west wing of the Ensor Estate. The mansion was a remarkable feat of architecture with its tall ceilings, large windows, and luxury finishes and furnishings. It had all the latest technological features, yet elegant chandeliers, velvet drapes, and sweeping staircases kept the sense of splendor. Nova stood in awe of the majesty of the house. Vizier Ida Watts had thought of everything down to the intricate details. In the Legacy Hall, paintings hung from floor to ceiling. Each collection of images was dedicated to preserving the history of Ida Watts and her renaissance.

Nova dipped the tip of her bush in blue paint. She loved the rubbery, plastic-like smell. It reminded her of her childhood. Her mom had always made sure they had art supplies stocked up.

"I miss her." Nova thought as she colored the space between the black lines on the wall. Her job was simple: write history, record, paint, and make it art. Three-fourths of the way down the hall, her brush stroked the wall repeatedly.

She couldn't help but think, "How did it all come to this?" The design of the city was still intact. The buildings rose in beauty. The architecture stunned her. Trees actually grew in the Dome and lined paths, and the flower clock bloomed in the Ensor Gardens. But a dark cloud of loneliness had fallen over the Fractal City of Eliora as Ida Watts led.

Marriages that once shone like the sun's rays now hid in the shadows. Not only had the government taken over daily parts of work life, but they were also interfering with relationships in the name of Tolerance.

Nova's brush colored the foreground and the background. The theme was meant to be inspiring, but the beige and blue colors were gloomy.

"I wonder if my mom would have eventually been given this kind of house," Nova considered the homes the Vizier allotted to each elderly woman. Blue shadows darkened the edges of the two-story square house Nova painted. Nova took three steps back to look at her work.

"Four hallways, check. Six bedrooms, check. Built into the city wall, check. The top story looks good." She brushed a strand of blonde hair away from her eyes. "The lower level's courtyard needs more color by the fountain," she thought, tilting her head to get a different angle.

Nova daydreamed about stepping into one of the beautiful courtyards opening from the living quarters.

"This is so different from the homes I've known. I mean, it provides for everyone." Nova imagined a grandmother rocking, a child playing with a doll, a poor woman resting, and a disabled woman being cared for.

"I guess people don't feel marginalized. Ida honors the elderly and lets them educate the grandchildren." The thought of her grandmother caring for her well-being made her laugh. "I would have loved that, and I'm pretty sure I would have driven her nuts. Granny, one more game of Chutes and Ladders."

Soon, a gold frame would wrap around the matrilineal family house that Nova painted. And if the walls could talk and the house could come to life, Nova would have seen each twelve-year-old child being assigned their own room at the Seer's yearly ceremony in the city gates, and the Vizier's new mating system would begin afresh.

Nova painted history even though she was just discovering it. She didn't fully understand Ida's systems until she had to paint their details. Coloring domestic settings, sketching wooden bedchambers honoring walking relationships made her want to avert her eyes. She didn't want to think about the fact that each night, a man could visit the bedchamber of any woman who had been given their own room at twelve years old.

"No one can be monogamous." Nova slumped.

"But..." the painting argued, "The good news of Ida's system was that it ensures that, in time, there would be no illegitimate children."

Nova sketched little boys over the age of two being placed in their mother's homes. They were not affected by the final solution of the Tolerance Law.

"If only my brother would have been two." A reel of still shots replayed in her mind: the river, the dock, her father... Nova closed her eyes. Ida did not allow any fatherly role where men were forced to provide for and protect their biological children. Instead, she put fewer responsibilities on men due to the city's war-torn past.

"My dad." A deep ache grew into yearning. "And now Alister is gone. When will I see him again?" A dark emptiness grew in his absence.

In the city, men and women worked their daily assignments on equal footing, but mothers held primary responsibility for the children. Inevitably, uncles and brothers became functional fathers within the matriarchal homes, but the role was always voluntary.

Ideas stacked up in Nova's to-paint pile as the Vizier strove to leave a legacy where people saw the Fractal City of Eliora as the great giving mother.

"Paint the city as a mother."

"Encourage citizens to honor the principles of care, love, and generosity." The notes went on and on.

"I love that the marginalized are cared for in Eliora, but are men the enemy?" Nova thought about the rules as her brush stroked the canvas. "Aren't they being pushed to the side now?" Thoughts of Alister filled her mind. "He gave me his own food." She remembered the sweater he had passed through the fence. How many nights had it kept her warm? "He taught me everything he knew. He never treated me like I was lesser. Now, should I rise at his expense?"

The Vizier's ideas grew into a stack of papers. Society spun like a top on a table. Nova, along with each citizen, must decide whether she would keep turning with her culture's laws or risk keeping an ancient tradition.

"Will I ever be able to marry? Is there a world where two people can live peacefully, honoring each other?" She felt Alister's words replaying, asking the same question, "Will you marry me?"

"How did it come to this? Marriage is against the law." Nova repeated it to herself nearly twenty times that day. Her eyes wandered down the long hall.

How did history wind up here? Her brush stroked the edge of the wall.

"Can history be rewritten, or is this how it should be?" Questions bounced around Nova's mind.

"Is marriage worth dying over? Is it worth being labeled intolerant?" Memories intruded. She heard the splashing river under her parents' bodies. She remembered her brother's newborn cry. Questions invaded her brain, "What if they do that to me? Or worse, Alister." Worrying thoughts came. Each sloshed around inside. Amid the fear, an ache for his companionship cracked open in her heart.

"I don't want a walking relationship— a different man here today and gone tomorrow. I want a commitment." Nova glanced at golden frames and red paint spread inside the lines. "What if true freedom isn't boundariless?" Nova tilted her head and pressed her lips together as she looked at the art.

"I don't want access to every man. I want *this* man. I want Alister." Nova wanted his words; He knows all of our inside jokes." She imagined his hand holding hers when times were tough.

When society changed, and everybody sought the right answer, Nova wanted greater love. She wanted his stability when the tyranny of men fell, when the tyranny of women fell, and when humanity fell. She clasped her hands at the nape of her neck.

"I want a child with his dark eyes." Nova dared to dream. The idea planted itself deep inside her mind and grew. At that moment, she decided Alister would be enough for her. "One man is enough. One Sovereign is enough. Being one is enough."

Nova knew what she had to do. But setting out at night, whispering to the man in a sewer drain, releasing its lid, and escaping into the underground with her lover would be more complicated than she thought now that she was in the city. First, she'd need to leave this hallway and find a way to cross radiation barriers. Scared but determined, Nova put down her paintbrush and took the first step.

12

"Get into your flats!" A Nomarch yelled in the street. Nova pushed the paintbrush deeper into her bag and quickened her steps. Thankfully, her flat was within walking distance from the Legacy Hall. She rushed past one of Eliora's famous landmarks, a statue of the crystal key, and cut onto a side street. Passing a flashing billboard, it caught her eye— the Vizier had declared a state of emergency. "Radiation is on the rise. Get into your homes," a Nomarch repeated.

Mere weeks into her work in the city, a developing radiation pandemic locked her up in her flat.

"Surely, this will pass in a couple of weeks." Nova considered it all as she shut the door behind her, "In the Outlands, didn't Officer Shaw say they were repairing cracks in the Dome?" Nova dropped her keys on the kitchen counter and sat on the couch. "I'm glad they're protecting people from the radiation." She remembered boils on her arms and thought about Emma racing toward the bathroom after crossing over the red line in the Apothecary. "I wouldn't wish that on anyone," she thought. "And it might be easier to get around the city if Nomarchs aren't patrolling every street corner." She told herself. "I'd have to figure out how to get iodine to cross the barriers. Maybe I could get to Alister."

The news on television flashed images of how the "Red Death" plague began to manifest itself in many forms in different people. Nova already knew this could happen because Emma had responded differently to the radiation than she had. She wrapped a blanket around herself on the couch and watched the news.

"Please do not leave your homes for any reason until we give further instructions," the news anchor directed.

Because of the citywide lockdown, no one left their flats or filled the streets. No one came knocking except isolation. Nova found herself alone, thinking, "How can I get to him?"

***

Early the following day, noise from the flat below snuck through Nova's second-floor window like a robber, stealing the silence. She breathed softly—eyes closed. The noise tiptoed around her room until it reached out to touch her dream. Nova's eyes split open. Nova's dream plagued her as it flooded her mind with images and ideas. She sat up, right-angled. "Ay!" Nova ran her fingers through her tumbleweed hair. Struggling, she murmured a list: "Yellow sun, white dress, red river, blue uniform."

Barely aware of where she sat, she whispered, "Decode the dream." Nova's eyes were swampy, thick, and heavy. Rain splashed on the window, and dirty-colored light spilled across the floor. Nova's warm hand pushed the quilt aside, forming a mound at the end of the bed. Nova's feet met the cold wood floor. The phrase from the dream replayed in her mind, "This is our delivery."

The next night, Nova barely slept as thoughts circled. No matter the mental path she took to finding Alister, it always came back to being caught. The Vizier's night watch still haunted the misty streets of Eliora. Radiation barriers lined certain parts of the city. Devising a plan proved frustrating, especially with the lockdown. Just standing on the street corner could get her arrested. Nova sat on her bed, thinking about the note Alister had snuck to her through the underground workers.

Remember the Outlander's song;

All will bloom in the Hour of the Lily
in the garden center.
A star's spark will light the throne

of the rightful heir.
A leaf will fall,
but roots go down deep.
The gift is the key
that will open the door.
Look for a son among the people.
Ask him to set his people free.

She stopped reading because Emma stood in the doorway. Nova popped straight up and gasped,

"Emma!" She closed the space between them and threw her arms around her friend.

"I couldn't stay away forever." Emma laughed and hugged her friend tight. "Here!" Closing the door, Emma dropped a note into Nova's hand.

"I got this at work today. Alister's crew was working in the underground by Second Street Bakery, and they managed to get this to me. He's coming for you, Nova!"

Nova's shaking fingers unfolded the note. Her lips curled into a smile. Alister had sketched a pencil drawing of a lily in the bottom right corner.

13

The next night, Nova clutched Alister's scribbled note. Under the Outlander's song, he wrote, "Meet me tomorrow under the Ember Bridge at 11 p.m." The secret meeting started in five minutes. Her steps quickened as she left The Fractal City's tall buildings behind. Pavement turned to grass as she passed through the Artisan Gate. She watched the ground for the red glow of a radiation barrier and avoided each one. Ahead, a lamp post illuminated the Ensor Gardens. Nova surveyed the green lawn; several protruding gray rocks were tall enough to climb on. Perfectly spaced Elm trees bordered the grass.

"Wow, actual growth," Nova whispered to herself. "And color, they are so green." Tilting her head heavenward, she found the darkness of the sky strange. The city often hid the celestial sphere in its orange glow. Each night at her flat, the street lights glimmered between the cracks of the curtains. She had only seen darkness like this in the Outlands.

Nova paused under the arc of Ember Bridge—an ornate iron bridge that stood southeast of the Artisan Gate. The walking bridge spanned Cullen path, where people liked to jog.

Cold air whirled under the bridge. Nova wished she had brought a jacket. The scar on her left arm began to ache.

"I need to watch for radiation barriers." She rubbed her wrist, trying to get rid of the pain. Nova tugged the edges of her sleeves down and stuffed her hands in the pockets of her ruby grid dress—a minute marched by. Nova turned around. Her fingers restlessly fidgeted with the gum wrapper she discovered in her pocket. Two minutes passed by. "Any time now," she assured herself. "Any minute." Nova started biting her nails. Five minutes. The silence grew louder until it was deafening. "Something is wrong. What if..." Her mind swelled with questions. "What if he doesn't come? What if I get caught?" A river burbled in the distance. The wind caught the leaves and swirled them. Crossing her arms over her chest, Nova backed towards the wall, wondering if it was the first sign of a storm. She sank into the shadows and froze. A twig snapped behind her, and a shadow shifted until it stretched across the ground. Someone grabbed her mouth before she could turn around and pulled her back firmly. A man's body forcefully pressed against hers. She felt his hot breath on the back of her neck. His rapid breathing exhaled by her ear. Nova's mouth muted, and her eyes darted back and forth, screaming. Nova's heart thumped wildly inside her chest—trying to escape.

"Quiet," the predator growled, face colored red. Nova's skin turned cold and clammy. That feeling of being trapped—suddenly she was there again—like it was yesterday: Sterile navy walls overlooked the spotless floor.

Medical beds lined a long triangle-shaped room. IV drip lines, with bags of fluid, hung beside each bed. Nomarchs stood stiff at attention, guarding the doors. The judge's verdict— contaminated Outlander! Then, the Nomarch's words, "Lie on the table."

Nova was pulled back into the present moment when she saw footsteps scuffing up dirt on the far side of the bridge. Her body felt heavy. Her sight narrowed to a pinprick. A man in a black uniform marched forward. The Nomarch wore a red cuff band on his left arm, black boots, and a peaked cap. His German Shepherd kept pace on his leash. Ears pointed, and the dog sniffed around. Nova tried to make sense of the situation. "Why is he out during this lockdown?" The dog's golden legs paused. His black snout rose high in the air. Did the wind carry her scent?

Nova gulped. Small, uneven gasps escaped her throat. The man's fingers tightened, curling around her mouth. His fingernails dug into her narrow cheeks. Nova's eyes burned in a strangled expression as the man forced her to remain motionless.

The Nomarch patrolling the Central Gardens tugged the dog's leash, and he trotted along. Soon, they disappeared beyond the side of the bridge.

"Alister sent me," a raspy voice whispered. "There are too many patrols tonight. It is not safe here." The man released his grip, "Go to 104 B Street." Nova slowly turned. The man watched her eyes grow in recognition. "No questions, Nova. You have to go!"

14

Nova set out for B street with quivering legs. A full moon was sewn perfectly into the blackened sky, stitched behind gray billowing clouds. Nova crouched behind thick trees. When the coast was clear, She moved quickly and focused on her footwork. Each heel-to-toe rolling movement muffled the sound of her steps. "Don't be afraid," she scolded herself. "It only draws attention." Nomarchs can sense anxiety. "Don't be a target."

In The Fractal City of Eliora, the buildings appeared glued together. Each structure fit together like small pieces of a jigsaw puzzle. Nova made record time while keeping close to the walls. She strained her eyes, searching for 104.

Nova was halfway down the street when a stormy mass of clouds coiled and writhed above the dome. Thunder cloaked the night. Rain drizzled through a filtration system over the city. It dripped off the cathedral's umbrella-shaped roof and landed on the cobblestone street, forming tiny rivers. Each one flowed in the grooves between the bricks. The huffing wind grew stronger as Nova darted through the lane with a sheet of pelting rain pursuing her. It made a buzzing noise, like a hoard of angry bees.

Each foot patted the ground and left a slight depression. Splashing up—beads of water burst up. Puddles rippled in the downpour.

Breathing deeply, Nova glanced over her shoulder.

"Is someone following me?"

The old streets once welcomed visitors. A canopy of string lights illuminated city life. Children once kicked balls in the street while aproned shopkeepers talked to customers. Displays showed off merchandise: shoes, dresses, watches, and wallets. In those days, men walked with their families to a massive cathedral on the corner of 2nd and B Street. Everyone came and went as they pleased. Most weeks, children raced off ahead of their parents to greet their friends, eager to make an exchange in the latest trading card game before service started.

But since the Vizier put The Tolerance Law into effect and mandated a quarantine, crossing into the Estelle only felt hauntingly sad. 104 B Street hid on the outskirts of Estelle, but Nova remembered her head pounding as the Thought Leaders hammered the Vizier's decree to the doors of the gutted cathedral at the very center.

***

A wave of relief flooded Nova when she finally saw the muddied side door of a dimly lit chapel under the label 104. Turning the brass knob, Nova left behind a row of foggy street lamps. Complaining loudly, the door behind her creaked to a close. Her mousy face glanced over her shoulder, uneasy. But even if her jittery hands would have held the key, the lock couldn't evaporate the threat that hunted her.

Immediately, Nova's eyes met the face of a man about twenty-three, with a heavy brown beard and ruggedly handsome features. She made for the front of the church to meet him. Alister smiled warmly, disarming fear's haunting artillery. Teeth chattering, she melted into his embrace.

"You're so cold." He squeezed her tighter. Carson Reed, the groundskeeper of the chapel, emerged from the shadows of the pulpit, his black blazer accentuating his ebony hair.

"You made it." Carson shifted a black book into his left hand.

"Sorry for the change."

"We got word of a new night patrol," Alister said worriedly. "In the Ensor Gardens. It was too close to the Ember Bridge."

Carson fiddled with his book. "Hit any trouble?"

Nova wrapped her arms around herself, still mildly shaking. Alister slipped off his white jacket and tended to her. His heavy coat cradled her as it draped over her narrow shoulders. The frigid air couldn't penetrate the barrier of the Merino white wool cloak. Nova swiveled to face Alister.

"Rain," Nova answered. "But honestly, I was thankful the noise hid the sound of my steps." Alister nodded. Nova's eyes squinted,
"But...it has done wonders to my *wedding* hair." She pursed her lips—pouting. "As my mother would say, I look like a drowned rat." Grinning, the group laughed, but the water kept dripping off the ends of her long blonde hair.

It was good to see everyone smiling. It was good to see people together. With the Red Death spreading because of the radiation barriers, Nomarch enforced laws that pushed people into their homes.

But today, everyone celebrated. Gwyn, garden architect and groundskeeper of the Ensor Gardens, ceremonially danced forward, carrying a blanket of hand-sewn shapes. Even after eleven years of a secret marriage, Gwyn's dark eyes still captured Carson's attention.

"Several friends who fear the Sovereign contributed a swatch of bright fabric for your union gift," Gwyn said, holding out the quilt. "Everyone wishes they could be here."

"Thank you," Nova said, admiring the vibrant quilt. Hundreds of tiny triangles and hexagons made up a lattice pattern.

"The artistry!" Nova's eyebrows arched in fascination. "The angle makes it seem like I'm looking through a wicket fence."

"Straight into a beautiful garden." Alister finished her sentence.
Nova glanced up, beaming, "This is truly amazing, Gwyn."

"Yes, you are quite the artist." Alister agreed, nodding.

"It was fun to make." The lattice provided a strong structure for the quilt's design. It revealed a protected beauty— showing the garden's absolute wonders: color, life, air, and light.

"Quickly now," Carson whispered.

"Yes, we don't have much time," Gwyn added. Empty pews materialized an imaginary audience as Alister and Nova took their place at the altar.

"Oh, wait," Gwyn whispered. She quickly pinned back the sides of Nova's long golden hair.

"A little surprise." She pulled out a fresh flower headdress—lush with greenery, berries, and roses that matched her ruby dress. She crowned Nova's head. Alister took hold of both of Nova's hands.

"You are beautiful." He could not hide his smile, "So beautiful." Nova focused her eyes, trying to shake away a twinge of panic. It was absurd since no one had burst through the door. She was sure no one had followed her. But it didn't make a difference; just being there was an act of resistance, a simple act that could be punished by death or a lifetime in the Outland's labor camps. Her crimson dress hung damp. Alister's wool jacket hung heavy on her shoulders. Nova's lungs expanded with strained air.

"Are you ready to make your vow?" Carson asked. If Alister had known discouragement or fear before this moment, it did not show. Everything from how he held himself to how Nova fell in step behind him said that he was the perfect leader for her. How he spoke and the intense confidence in his brown eyes assured her. She trusted Alister. Time after time, he had sacrificed for her good. In the Outlands, he had listened to her. They shared common beliefs and values. Marriage was a risk Nova would take.

After a small collection of minutes, the couple covenanted themselves to one another, and as surely as dust and decay would meet their mortal bodies, God became their witness.

On that white-dressed winter night, a love story unfolded with lines of laughter, singing, prayer, and risk. In the flickering candlelight, the great Artist knit together two separate lives— lacing diversity into unity.

Man and woman were bound together in a new web of life. Around each corner lay a fresh story of oneness. Each word of commitment stitched together an intricate design, weaving a beautiful tapestry on the foundation of love. Whether sickness or health, poverty or wealth would touch their home in the coming days, they did not know, but the rings that encircled their fingers held the hope that their love would endure until death parted them. Man and wife stood face to face with their backs to the world.

Alister's hands rested softly on her neck. Nova's pulse beat faster, her heart flowing with warmth. He brushed back her hair. In the dim light, he saw her beauty. Alister drew close until his warm lips found hers. Heart mingled with soul—swaying until the world fell silent. Rays of love, youth, and beauty shone all around. Nova lost track of all time and space as joy and wonder danced, suspending her in that moment. A kiss became their crowning act of defiance.

15

By 1 a.m., the isolated street outside the chapel lay eerily quiet. Under a charcoal sky, the city slept. The streetlights, like soldiers, stood at attention. Avoiding their watchful eyes, Nova dreaded their flashes of light, the whistle blow, the chase.

"We'll have to take different routes to be less likely to be seen." Alister reminded her where to turn.

"Ok. I'll be right behind you." Nova waited for the changing of the guards before heading out. Following the map in her head, Nova counted her steps. Footprints left brief impressions—a trail of fleeting shadows. The wind whispered in her ear. She pulled her coat tighter and promised herself ten more steps. She told herself, "Just ten more."

Reaching the fractal corner, Nova paused at E Street and 5th Avenue. She turned down a narrow side street and faced the biting wind.

Traveling down a narrow alleyway, Nova avoided patches of ice from yesterday's rain. Mice scattered near her feet in search of food. The brick walls stared at her, silent and expressionless. Icy air burned her lungs, and each breath formed a cloud. Nova's arms felt weighted down by icy veins. She walked on.

A wooden hatch slumped against the brick wall. Bending down, Nova yanked. The door, protesting the chill, creaked until it opened. Pale stairs, rather sick-looking, hid underneath. "Only five steps to safety." Nova couldn't resist the urge to smile. Nova left behind the murky snow piles, the passive buildings, and the gray-tinted air as she entered a secret storage room.

The circular drain hid under a rug as Alister said it would. As Nova disappeared into the underworld, the grate resumed its place.

***

The Ensor Gardens were a work of art with paths outlining different garden lawns. Each had a bench that overlooked the grounds.

"That is the flower clock Gwyn takes care of," Alister whispered, pointing to the budding flowers in a greenhouse.

"Each flower blooms at a different hour," he whispered. The fourth hour held roses. Elegant lilies filled the eleventh-hour slot. As a garden architect, Gwyn knew that the flower's official name was "Lilium Tigrinum," but she called it the tiger lily like everybody else. She took joy in coining the eleventh-hour "hour of the lily."

Spotted and bright as the tiger lily was, Nova was drawn to a white winter bulb. The star flower had six petals opening wide to reveal a yellow center.

"It's in full bloom." Nova crouched behind a tree.

"It's eleven." Alister shifted on his feet. "We need to get to the Glistening Tree."

Nova stepped out. Ahead, the Glistening Tree's leaves moved as if juggling secrets of the past, present, and future. Leaves pulsed with orange, yellow, and red. It lit up like a match had struck the tree and ignited it. Magic flowed through each branch down into each leaf. The magic held a tiny triad of birth, life, and death as a leaf fell from the branch to the ground. All consumed, Nova stared at it like it was the bridge between heaven and earth.

"It's magic. I mean, compared to the wasteland we are used to. It's Majestic. Beautiful." Nova drew closer to the tree, removing her shoes, needing to feel the earth under her feet.

"How does it live?" Nova felt its vibrations and clutched her heart.

"I haven't seen anything like this, even in the Dome?" Alister added in amazement. "We put the key here," Alister pointed to a knot in the bark. Pulling out the key, Alister reached it toward the knot. Nova watched breathlessly as the tree changed when Alister turned the crystal key. The bark rearranged itself, revealing a small opening. It grew larger and larger until the couple could step inside the tree. Nova walked through the magical force. Was it pulling her? Her eyes flicked down to her arms. The surface of her wounded skin drained. The pain was relieved as her skin transformed, smoothing over. Slack-jawed, Nova stared, unable to move. Alister's eye crinkled as he smiled.

A brilliant light illuminated a set of steps inside the tree and swallowed up the darkness.

"This way." Alister pointed. One step turned into two, then four, then eight. Nova traveled down the long flight of steps deeper inside the tree. Never looking back, she followed her husband forward. The staircase reached deep into the roots. On the wall, an ornate sconce emitted sparks of light. The orange light bulb flickered like a firefly. When she reached the bottom of the stairs, the couple stood in a root cellar.

***

The last week leading up to the wedding had been the hardest. Nomarchs secretly invaded houses, stole land, and discarded even more sons. The Vizier recruited neighbors to report pregnancies and births. Parents must spin the wheel of fortune after a live birth. Citizens no longer dragged murder into court; the jury was simply a choice.

In the darkness, time froze for the lovers. In the damp root cellar of the Glistening Tree, Alister and Nova resisted. They had chosen marriage. Still, with everyone caught up in Tolerance and ever-expanding building projects, there was little talk of anyone's future.

Time had never stopped during Nova's day-to-day routines in the city. Each day, Nova's thoughts and expectations piled up as she painted at home for the Legacy Hall. She wondered when everything would return to normal, but she never dared to ask, "When will this radiation pandemic end? When will I be allowed to marry freely?" She only thought, "Oh! If only we could live through this. If only we could stay together and somehow live." The thoughts came every day; everyone secretly thought them. She prayed but rarely mentioned it. A strange silence engulfed her, and now she stood alone with Alister for the first time since they were kids.

Alister tried to act normal to set Nova at ease, but the fear of what could come lingered around the edges of the root cellar. The darkened corners whispered, "Will they discover you? Will you meet again?"

In the dim light, Alister smiled, igniting butterflies in Nova's stomach. An intense feeling of joy silenced the fear. The intense involuntary attraction pulled them together. Alister leaned down and kissed his wife.

"I don't even have words," Nova said, smiling as she rested safely in his arms.

"Will you have courage?" He smiled.

Nova retorted, "What kind of man marries a woman when the government is allowed to murder their children?"

"What kind of woman says yes?" He winked. "Deliverance will come." Alister was resolute—not afraid of the Vizier's edict. They both knew the coming weeks could separate them, miles might spread them apart, but nobody could steal tonight. In that broken-down cellar, enclosed by The Fractal City, the stars glistened above and reflected on the city's wide river.

"I'm going to build you a home." Alister smiled.

"When the radiation pandemic ends?" Nova grimaced, listening to her own words. She had dared to dream, and longing spilled out. Alister picked up an abandoned brick and a cracked bucket.

"Tonight!" He marked four corners of an imaginary house. The architect went to work designing a floor plan. Alister pointed out the make-believe front door. Nova smiled, hanging a pretend evergreen wreath on it. He started the tour, pointing out each new room as he stepped through them. By the time he finished, Nova was on her feet, smiling. Alister led her in, pausing to carry her—his bride over the threshold. The edges of her dress swept through the air as she came home.

Nova sat on an overturned apple crate. Alister stooped to whisper. They dreamed up a set of red armchairs in their imaginary house next to a lit fire. Books lined their shelves. Lights hung from the ceiling while pictures decorated the walls. Hot chocolate steamed from imaginary mugs. The blurry house came into focus, appearing like a mirage in the dusty cellar. At first, she could see through it, but soon enough, everything was solid.

    Alister kept Nova talking and made her laugh. Rows of dusty shelves eavesdropped. Cobwebs watched. The smell of must lingered as the couple sat smiling in the middle of their dreamed-up cottage. An overturned crate transformed into their side table. A flickering candle lit the table, casting a shadow.

    "I have a present for you." Nova's eyes beamed like a child on Christmas morning. Alister pulled a package from the pocket of his jacket. Unraveling the brown paper, Nova smelled Second Street Bakery's fresh bread. Alister brought out slices of cheese and a small bottle of wine.

    Nova's heart burst at Alister's kindness. That moment held the happiest of lovers and forever marked their marriage. Alister grew dearer to her. Their playhouse was more real than any incredible architectural feats she had seen in The Fractal City, for they lived together in that moment under the real stars, with real bread, with real love. That night, hope was conceived before the baby ever was.

16

One day, the paint smell on her canvas made Nova's eyes cross. "I used to love this smell." She covered her O-shaped mouth and tried not to gag. But inevitably, the unsettling feeling grew in her stomach until she hung her head over the toilet.

Quarantine added a layer of protection for Nova's baby. With no one allowed out of their flats, Nova easily hid her morning sickness. Each day, she pulled out oil paints. Nova brushed abstract shapes and lines onto the canvas until city skylines and sunsets emerged from the colors. Her collection of finished canvases grew every week as she fulfilled her work quota from home.

Nova lay on the couch at noon. Her eyelids felt heavy, and she let herself momentarily doze off. Emma snuck into her flat through their adjoining door. She set a rare jar of pickles on the coffee table with a note from Alister. Emma tiptoed past Nova, careful not to wake her. Half an hour later, Nova's eyes blinked open. The muscles around Nova's eyes tightened at the sight of the miracle gift.

"Pickles!" Her cheeks lifted, and the sides of her lips rose. The sharp taste of vinegary salt water dripping off the end of the pickle satisfied the sour craving Nova had been experiencing for days. "Thank you; I don't know how you managed this with rationing," she mouthed as she chewed every crunchy morsel. Over time, Nova's belly grew tight until one day, a slight flutter kicked. Nova sighed, "Life." And the intrusive thought, "They want to kill you." It made her want to kick something. "How can they hate someone so small and unseen?"

Nova laughed when her stomach hiccupped, and it wasn't her. Most nights, Nova was convinced the baby practiced toe touches because no matter how she lay, the baby poked her in the ribs.

One night, Nova groaned in the darkness, "I'm a giant moose." Tears slid down her cheeks. Emotions swirled. One minute, she laughed, and the next, she sobbed into her pillow. Whenever her feelings rose, she reached for Alister's note and reread his words. He always knew how to encourage and reassure her even if he couldn't be there in person.

Still, her thoughts raced at times, "Why is everything in this flat so dirty? My baby is coming. I need a name. What am I going to do about diapers?" I need to organize my dresser. I'm so hungry. I hate *all* food. I'm so excited. This is so scary. Both arms stretched around her bump. "How am I going to keep you safe?"

***

Far below Nova's flat, a father turned down a different drain pipe than his crew. When no one saw him, he ran. Disappearing down a dark tunnel, Alister escaped, splashing through a thin layer of water.

"The old ruler hid the crystal key," Carson, the cathedral's groundkeeper, had told his friend. Alister replayed the conversation in his head.

"Only one patch of land grew after the nuclear war began. No one can figure out why it is unaffected by the radiation spills when everything else was left as a wasteland. But the garden thrived."

"So Ida saw the good land and took it," Alister had said.

"Yes, she built the city around the Glistening Tree and the flower clock, and what's weird is that she is oblivious to the fact that it seems to help people. It has the exact opposite effect of the radiation. Take Gwyn, for example. When she works in the garden every day, her sight improves. But in her flat in the city wall, where the radiation is stronger, it's harder for her eyes to focus. She sits at the piano and says the sheet music is blurry."

Alister grinned, remembering the conversation. He rubbed his hands together as he neared the Ensor Gardens. A steel rim of a drain grate lay above him. It creaked and popped open as he pressed against it. Alister pulled himself up into the city's garden. Green grass anchored its roots in the soil, making a lush-trimmed lawn. The breeze carried the delicate smell of lavender. The Ensor Gardens were just as majestic as he remembered. As Alister stood before the flower clock, a squirrel scurried to a nearby tree. White lilies bloomed. Their fragrance carried a honeyed-earthy aspect.

Alister knelt. His fingers reached into the petals of a little trumpet. In the center of the lily, he plucked out the crystal key and laid it in the palm of his hand.

The aged Glistening Tree's orange shining leaves crackled. Rustling bright foliage moved in the presence of the father. Alister curled his fingers around the cold key and twisted it into the keyhole on the tree's knob.

The father got to work immediately. He cleared away moss-veiled rocks, thinking of his bride. Twigs crunched under his feet as he imagined his child. He swept the leaf-carpeted ground to make a path. Like a woodpecker, he drummed deeper into the tree's roots, making room after room for his house. He prepared a place for his wife and child. Day after day, night after night, he worked tirelessly. Sweat beaded his forehead, but the hours passed like minutes when he thought about bringing his family home. As long as the quarantine held up, he had time to prepare.

One night, deep in the root cellar, he dreamed. A bell chimed on Nova's bicycle. Her blonde hair blew in the wind as she rode down a narrow cobblestone street. Yellow light flickered through the trees lining the river. Birds chirped in their branches. Someone grabbed her wrist.

A burly man stood at the end of the alleyway. He grabbed a book from a wheelbarrow and tossed it into a crackling fire. Nova's hand reached for a rope and pulled. Bells rang overhead. A shadow grew over her white dress. A group of people gathered by the river, all clapping and cheering. Alister heard a splash. Blood painted the river red. Someone unfamiliar spoke, "Stop them!" A man in a navy uniform blew his whistle and barked, "Don't let one of them get away." Nova ran. Rounding the corner, she felt a twinge of pain. Blinking wildly, she slid to sit down. Holding her rounded belly, Nova winced and wiped the sweat from her brow. Alister placed his hand on Nova's shoulder, then gave her a swaddling blanket—their union gift.

Alister whispered, "This is our delivery."

Alister's eyes darted open. He paused, heart pounding. "It was so full of color, yet all so...gray." Alister rubbed his hand through a scruff of hair. "I need to get her out. This is a warning."

17

The radiation quarantine ended just as suddenly as it started. Hearing a knock, Nova opened the front door. Two Nomarchs stood stiff.

"Let me see your wrist." Nova held out the star-shaped scar on her wrist.

"Nova Bromley, you are under arrest for committing Amity. Reported under the Neighbors Law, you have the right to remain silent. Anything you say can be used against you in a court of law."

Handcuffs tightened against Nova's wrists. Nine months of dealing with morning sickness, quarantining in a radiation pandemic, and having weird cravings all came to a crashing halt. The earthquaking reality shook Nova. She knew she could not protect her baby forever, but the quarantine had kept her secluded this far. How was this happening so soon?

"We are taking your baby." The Nomarch's simple words shattered the tiny universe holding her child.

Nova hunched over in pain—feeling the shattering thrust, the expulsion, the displacement. How could her child be taken away to a matriarchal harem or hear the spinning wheel of fortune?

Nova could think of nothing to say. In her lamblike silence, a cramp surged through her belly, hardening it like a rock. She bleated, making inhuman noises. A blinding flash covered her mind as she tried to grasp what was happening. Her world spun, and no one could see it.

Two armed Nomarchs tightened the handcuffs when she should have danced at the thought of new life. At that moment, Nova felt an internal lurch. She heard a slight pop, and watery fluid gushed onto the floor.

"We need an ambulance," Emma yelled, appearing in the hallway.

***

The birth personnel stopped the ambulance in front of the Birth Center. Hurrying, two paramedics lay Nova on a stretcher and wheeled her through the automatic double doors of the birth center. The wheels on the stretcher rattled. Emma took heavy steps beside Nova as they rushed in.

"Ma'am. You can't follow them." The receptionist's hand reached out to stop Emma. She pushed through. "Ma'am. You must stop." Two armed security guards stepped in front of her, building a barrier. Her eyes raced down the hallway after her friend. Nova couldn't see much but noticed Emma's balled fists dangled by her side. Her teeth clenched. Her jaw fixed firm. She stared unblinkingly. Nova couldn't read her mind but saw the tears filling her eyes.

Nova's face creased as Emma disappeared behind her. A fog of anxious thoughts surrounded Nova. "What if it is a boy?" "How can I escape? What will my future be?" The heavy rumble of a turning wheel droned into her thoughts. "Who will deliver me?"

"Ahhh." Nova twisted her body, trying to get comfortable. A cramp surged through her stomach, hardening like a rock. Lost inside of herself, she winced until the contraction leveled off. At the end of the hospital corridor, she arrived in a private ward—CleanRoom 206.

Sighing, Nova lay back and pulled up her knees. She adjusted the stiff pillow. Nova closed her eyes. The lights were too bright. And the air had an underlying smell of bleach—enough to make anyone feel nauseous.

The paramedic's name, Taylor Vource, was inscribed on a gold name badge. A logo of a snake slithering up a pole was engraved next to his name. He avoided eye contact. Too occupied to look at Nova, he scanned her chart. The room felt too cold, too clinical. When he approached her bed, his shoes stuck to the floor. A little sucking sound accompanied each step. He tightened a numbered band around her wrist.

"Would you like a twilight sleep?"

"What? What is that?" Nova questioned.

"Morphine and scopolamine. The side effect is you won't remember the birth." The thin atmosphere filled with unease. Nova shook her head,
"No."
"Suit yourself."
When the birth personnel wheeled her past twenty-six fractal pods in the west wall, she couldn't help but notice one of the paramedic's pockets—full of straps, seatbelts, or something. A contraction suddenly turned the hospital room inside out as pain crested over Nova's rounded belly.

"Put this on." Battling severe pain, Nova surrendered to the strong garment that slipped over her head. As she breathed deeply, the room finally reappeared—standing upright. The garment had long sleeves sewn shut. The paramedic crossed Nova's arms and confined them in front of her. The straight jacket was too tight. Rough hands fastened the belts on the back as another contraction started. The man stretched out her legs, oblivious to Nova's pain. Metal buckles clinked as the belt secured her ankles. Nova noticed the five o'clock shadow on the paramedic's face. How many times had he done this? Nova wondered. Leather loops surrounded her arms. Securely fastened to the bed, Nova was not going anywhere.

"The midwife will be in shortly," he voiced—deep and indifferent. As he stepped away, the door connecting to the hallway banged to a close. Just as quickly as it closed, it opened.

A midwife—short with dark hair—walked in carrying a metal tray. Unhurried, the midwife ceremonially checked the contamination level in the room. The Birth Center was nothing like Nova had imagined. She was a caged animal: no windows, just bare walls.

The white tiled ceiling was the only thing to look at. The cement floor lay helpless and gray—looking somewhat depressed. Next to Nova's bed, a one-legged stand held a computer—constantly monitoring her. It spit out a ribbon of paper. A strand of bedraggled hair landed on her sweating forehead.

"Ahhh." Nova's eyes narrowed. She wanted to hunch over so badly. Her eyes flooded with pain-filled tears when her baby was about a minute away from entering the world.

"Boy...ah..." she moaned. "What if it is a boy?" Pale walls surrounded her, leaning in to watch the birth. The midwife, uniformed in a white dress, black shoes, and sterilized gloves, pulled out a fresh blanket.

"Push," she instructed. The monitor beeped, and the IV bag dripped. Nova pressed her lips tight. The world pulled back, and it was so quiet she could almost hear a ringing noise.

Relief flooded, and suddenly, her pain began to ease. Nova sighed heavily. Silence hid the voice behind the medical mask. The midwife's deep, ebony eyes widened as she attended to the baby.

On this day, the 13th of December, the Vizier puts into effect the Tolerance Law. All male offspring produced under these conditions will immediately be discarded at the birthing center. Under penalty of....

The decree vibrated in Nova's mind. Thoughts of losing her baby brother to the edict twelve years earlier flashed like snapshots. She saw the little Moses basket sail into the open river. She remembered the breeze that chilled him to the bone. She remembered the silence of him not crying.

Air filled Nova's baby's lungs. An open-mouthed cry vibrated off the sterile walls. A single tear left a trail down Nova's cheek.

"It's a..." The midwife hesitated. "It's a male." Words locked themselves away. Nova's eyes widened. Her mouth froze open. The icy words weren't meant to be rude, but the air seemed to escape the room as Nova's heart beat heavily. She knew what that meant. And Nova was utterly unprepared for the growing anger that intertwined with despair.

Nova wished she felt like shouting or crying—anything to cause relief. But nothing came. She winced, thinking of the mother across the hall. Tomorrow, she would leave with a newborn swaddled in pink. Her arms would be full. What would she have?

Nova's imagination flashed images into her mind. She envisioned the removal, the wheel's spin, the blade of a knife, the river stained by his blood, and the dreaded moment when her baby would no longer cry. Nomarchs would force her to watch his arms and legs twitch until they lay motionless. His body would go limp. The seven-pound, eleven-ounce body would lie inactive on a table. The silence would be deafening.

Nova's eyes darted up, searching the midwife's face. She looked for even one glimmer of light. The midwife pinched her lips together as Nova waited for her to say something—"I'm going to take the baby now, let me get you cleaned up; you did well; it's over"— something. But she didn't speak; she just removed the IV. Nova's throat tightened, and it was hard to talk.

"He's beautiful." Her voice came close to noiselessness. "So fine."

Silence.

She wanted to kiss the baby's forehead.

"Tell me something," the midwife interrupted, "Because I don't understand. Why did you risk this? This law has been in place for over a decade." Nova felt a lump grow in her throat. Still strapped to the bed, a tear rolled down her face. The midwife's hand rested on her shoulder for minutes as the tears fell silently. The midwife watched until the baby started making noise. Nova swallowed the lump and looked up. The midwife stepped back. Nova wanted to wipe her eyes.

"I'm sorry," she sniffed. "When you've seen a history of spilled blood—a river dyed red; when you've heard an edict that says, "Make a choice," when you've felt the weight of a little body with a soul; when you've breathed in the wind that blows wherever it wishes; when you've tasted what it means to be a part of a family, then you'd know why I risk." Her eyes spoke loudly, "I'm not afraid of the edict."

The midwife's eyes darted left to right. Her face grew pale. Sweaty hands wiped the sides of her uniform. She leaned forward until they were inches apart.

"You were never a patient here." The midwife caught Nova's eyes and whispered quietly. Nova wasn't even sure she spoke. Nova studied the midwife's colorless face. Hands trembling, the nurse turned and faced the computer. The idea seemed ludicrous, but she repeated it a little louder this time, "You were never a patient here." She punched the backspace button.

"Do you understand me? You were never here."

The midwife crinkled the paper in her hand and ripped the medical report. She tore it into little white snowflakes. Each piece fell into the trash can. The midwife seemed weighed down by her own clothes; still, she leaned in nervously and loosened the strap on Nova's arm.

"I fear the Sovereign. I fear Him."

The midwife looked over her shoulder, almost expecting someone to appear. Then she turned her full attention to cutting Nova free. She looked Nova straight in the eyes.

"In my case, the authorities may take me, but you are a mother." The tiniest smile appeared. "This is your union gift. May he set our people free."

18

Darkness filled the alley behind the hospital. Nova's chest tightened with a burning sting. She crouched behind a trash can, waiting for the coast to be clear. Her flat in the west wall stood twenty-one blocks away. It might as well have been in another city with everyone out of the lockdown. Her back pressed against the brick building. With little time to plan, she moved toward 104 B Street. The midwife had securely wrapped the baby around Nova's chest, and her jacket safely covered him. "I have you back from the dead," Nova whispered as she looked into his deep eyes. When the grave opened its arms wide for him, and the gravestone readied itself to cover him, color filled his face. Stillness longed to kiss him but could not touch him in her embrace. He lived: his heart beat steadily next to hers, and his lungs expanded with air. The baby wiggled against her chest. Her tender words, "I love you," could have been their final words. Instead, her last words became first words. All of their lasts became firsts. Adrenaline flowed heavily through Nova's body. She walked forward like the sun that stayed its course. Tears wouldn't come. She couldn't stop until she knew her baby was safe. Racing along, she questioned, "What was this feeling of loss? This sudden joy? This life?" When she thought the sun was setting, Nova saw it dawning over the city. The mercy of a new morning blew all around her. The air filled her lungs, and she breathed deeply. She knew he wasn't hers to keep, but she had today, the present. Jude was the first boy to survive the Tolerance Law.

19

Tucked away in the Fractal City, behind locked doors of a chapel, Gwyn pulled out knobs on the organ. Her fingers danced across the ivory keys. Its mighty sound filled the whole cathedral. Her feet pressed the floor keys, playing those arrestingly deep notes. Five thousand pipes took turns singing and harmonizing. For a moment, Gwyn lost herself.

She glanced up at the hymnal. The music began to blur, becoming one big black note. One eye seemed to magnify all the notes, and the other eye saw everything from a distance. Her head began to ache. The radiation was getting stronger. Gwyn squeezed her eyes shut and played the rest of the song by heart. A knock came at the side door. Gwyn looked up. Opening the door, she found a soaked mother swaddling a child. Gwyn pulled her inside.

Nova pulled a crinkled letter from her pocket and handed it to Gwyn.

> *I am coming! I got word that the radiation levels are rising in the city. There are cracks in the Dome. We must get to the Glistening Tree to survive the coming radiation levels. The root cellar is ten feet underground. It will be a safe spot.*
> *Meet me at the Glistening Tree when the full moon rises in the hour of the Lily.*
> *Yours forever, Alister.*

"That's tonight," Nova said.

"Over here." Gwyn pointed to a panel on the pipe organ. She pushed it, which triggered a small door. A small room opened up. Pads lined the wall to block out noise. Nova could hear Gwyn's music, but it wouldn't blare in her ears.

"I've been working on this little place for months. Emma told me months ago that we'd need it." Gwyn smiled. Nova climbed into the secret room.

"We'll get your son to the tree in this." Gwyn emptied stationary out of a nearby basket. "I've collected iodine shots from the midwives for months. I put them over there in that corner. I'll be back tonight. We have to get to the Ensor Gardens by eleven." The tiny door shut, and the time of hiding began.

Every minute was a gift, each second a treasure. Feet shuffled across the wood floor. Nova stared into her son's eyes. Nova caressed his little head. Oh, the smell of newborn skin. She planted a gentle kiss on his forehead. The baby slept soundly. Minutes turned like pages, split, and fell open. Nova walked through time, finding her place in his story.

As the baby slept, the thought washed over Nova, "He isn't mine to keep." Tick. Tock. Her heart beat like a clock. Time marched on. As any mother would, she attentively watched his every breath. Nova longed for time to stop.

Outside the chapel, men hammered. Buildings grew into the sky. Determined to leave a legacy, the Vizier oversaw new bridges extending across the river. Nova cradled her baby, gently rocking him back and forth. The Vizier built walls. An aerial view of the city showed that the open areas became divided by hedges, buildings, and fences. Nova held her baby close. She was determined to build a different kind of legacy.

***

"Where is he?" Gwyn asked, looking up from her watch, "Carson is three minutes late." Nova tapped her foot and looked out the second-story window again. The gatekeepers at Entrance number six shifted. Was it already time for the changing of the guard?

"We n-need more time." Nova stuttered.

"We have to drop him now." Gwyn looked her in the eye.

"This could be your last chance." Nova rocked back and forth, making no response.

"You have to make it in time." Gwyn was right. Nova approached the window. It overlooked a wide road beneath. During the day, the street held heavy traffic; one man's load of boxes would shift and nearly spill. Another woman would race forward, holding an armful of vegetables. A truck driver would honk at them all. Too many people stood in his way. But at night, that general hum of activity died down.

Nova knew she couldn't keep Jude hidden forever. Reeds, bits of grass, willow, and bamboo made up the basket in her arms. A cream-colored blanket cushioned him. Nova snapped a picture in her mind: chubby hands, tiny nose, rosy cheeks, dark wisps of hair. His wide eyes looked up at her.

"Don't make this any harder than it has to be," she whispered. Her lips tightened as she wiped her eyes. "I love you." Gwyn wrapped her arms around Nova.

"Help me lift this basket." Gwyn fastened a rope around it. Nova fixed the lid shut. She paused, head hanging between her shoulders. Memories of her newborn brother intruded. Her hand rested on the basket, whispering a prayer,

"Sovereign... Please..." Nova bit her lip. They timed the escape perfectly so the changing of the guard wouldn't spot the basket. A string of questions filled Nova's mind. Would this unimpressive little basket turn her son's fortune? Would he live a long life? Why must Jude be thrown into such waves of adversity at a young age?

"There he is." Gwyn pointed. The delivery truck rumbled down the Street. Nova strained her eyes to see Carson on the empty street. Nova closed her eyes and sighed,

"He made it."

"Ok, you go first." Gwyn handed her the rope. Nova obeyed and climbed out the window, lowering herself.

"Ready?" Gwyn whispered.

"Yes," Nova replied. Gwyn lowered the basket as the guards stood at attention a moment longer. The basket approached the ground when its weight moved to one side. A corner of the rope snapped. Nova gasped and dove forward as the basket thudded to the ground. Jude whimpered.

Carson opened the back of the bakery food truck and quickly helped Nova with the basket. Nova sat beside the basket. Without a word, Carson jumped in the driver's seat. The wheels flowed through the rain's tiny rivers of water on the cobblestone street, carrying the Moses basket further away.

20

"Stop." A Nomarch held up his hand. Carson pressed his foot against the break. "What business do you have on Oort Street?"

Carson forced his head up, "Bread delivery."

"Stay calm," Nova thought as she took a deep breath in the back of the truck. "Act normal." She mouthed a prayer. "What if he cries?" She focused her eyes, "Stay calm."

"We search all vehicles after sundown," the Nomarch said. "Open the back." Nova's blood ran cold.

The bread truck's wheels gripped the cobblestone street as if bracing themselves. The revving engine died down. Carson's front door slammed. The click on the back door opened. Nova sat securely like a statue. She prayed. "Sovereign, please don't let him cry. Please, help him to be quiet."

A clean, slightly sweet, yeasty aroma came from the back of the truck. The Nomarch stepped through the opened doors into the bread truck. The butt of his gun pressed against several of the bakery racks. Nova tried to piece together what was happening. She looked down. "Don't look at the basket," she told herself. "Don't look at the basket." The Nomarch's black boots kicked against a bread tray. Sitting on a bench at the back of the truck, Nova flinched when the wheels of the bready racks squeaked. Glancing sideways, he watched her. His eyes narrowed, and he frowned.

"Step out while I look around." The Nomarch extended a finger to the door. Silence swelled between them. Turning slightly, Nova moved forward. Leaving her baby in a basket, not cradling him in her arms, in a way denying his existence, made time slow down. The baby's presence tortured Nova.

Outside the truck, nighttime held Nova in its dark clutches. She strained to eavesdrop on every noise coming from the back of the truck.

"Well, look at this." the Nomarch said.

**

A tight smile formed across the Nomarch's face. Nova whipped her head around, eyes darting. She bit her lip. Her fingers fidgeted.

"A Blueberry Streusel Muffin," the muffin didn't last long in his hand. He gobbled it hungrily. Crumbs fell to the floor. Nova smiled at the blueberry muffin in his hand. She let out a long, slow breath.

"No rationing me," the Nomarch said, crushing blueberries between his teeth. He stepped out and motioned them toward Second Street Bakery, following the bread truck with lust-filled eyes.

Bells chimed above the door of the bakery. It released steaming hot air full of buttery fumes. If not for the rationing, people would line up in droves from the sweet smell of cupcakes in the oven or the freshly baked loaves in the window.

Like a designer at work, Emma hardly noticed the door open but paid attention to every detail of the ingredients she added to the next bread batch. Emma's routine was like clockwork. Tired from her long shift, she wanted to flip the sign over to "closed." She had already packed the next day's ration orders, set up new fresh bread displays, and ensured the display cases were full.

"Carson!" Emma's eyes grew. "What are you doing here?" He glanced out the window at the truck.

"I need to make a delivery. That Nomarch is watching me."
Emma's eyes shifted to the Nomarch outside.

"Pull around back, Carson. It's ready for you." The Nomarch's gaze set Emma back to work. She immediately checked the baking ingredients and prepared the equipment for tomorrow's round of baking before getting the delivery. She checked the oven temperatures and started kneading, rolling, cutting, and shaping the last batch of dough. The steamy aroma followed Carson out the door. Forced to act normally, Emma couldn't help but worry about her friend.

As soon as the Nomarch was out of sight, Emma knew she would leave the bakery and not return home. Instead, she decided to meet her friends in the Ensor Gardens just like they had planned.

21

Carson opened the back of the truck. Nova held the basket in her arms.

"Sitara works in the back. She will help you from here."

"Thanks," Nova whispered. "Go. We don't want to draw the Nomarch's attention." The truck rumbled away. Grime stuck to the bottom of Nova's shoe as she moved to the bakery's back entrance. She wrestled the knob. Looking right and left, her stomach dropped when she realized it was locked. The alley smelled like a mixture of motor oil and leftover food from the neighboring restaurant's open windows. Steadying her hand on rough bricks, she used the wall to pull the jammed door—stuck!

Nova turned around. Down the back alley, signs hung over the back entrances of The Color Shop and Mr. Thayden's Suede Wonders. Wind shuffled bits of trash. A cat stepped over a dirty puddle and meowed. Looking around, Nova realized Tin Pan Alley lived a double life.

In full light, workers crinkled trash bags and slammed the bin lids down. Chattering people filled chic cafés, and their conversations echoed in the concealed alleyway. But after sunset, the dark side of the alley awoke. Open windows caught music that bounced off of The Velvet Room's back entrance. Pianos clamored for attention. The bluster and excitement always sounded like hundreds of people pounding on tin pans, which is how it got its name: Tin Pan Alley.

She didn't know it, but Nomarchs would soon step over broken glass in the alley to get to their secret meetings. Workers would take their smoke breaks and allow stray dogs to root through garbage. Mice would scamper away to hide. The side streets would no longer welcome its normal visitors.

Nova scanned the darkening alley. A canopy of string lights illuminated a brown dog sitting by a lamppost. The lab barked. A black snake's tale disappeared behind the dumpster, just out of the dog's reach. Nova's lungs burned as she breathlessly tried to open the door without making any noise.

The dog barked again. In the darkness, Nova's eyes filled. Drops fell from the clouds above. Nova couldn't get over the weather difference under the dome compared to the Outlands. This kind of rain was a novelty, and the sun a complete rarity compared to the Outland's snow and ice.

She wiggled the knob again. Nova's eyes widened when she realized the Cathedral looked over the corner of Tin Pan Alley. Rain dripped off its corners. Under nightfall, its roof seemed to sag a bit. In Tin Pan Alley, Nova found herself in the center of the Estelle, where rumors sparked and spread like wildfire. Each day, whispers grew louder: A neighbor disappeared. A child vanished. Nomarchs dragged a family to headquarters. The thought of the offices so near made her feel nauseous. The base of the operations building looked innocent enough under the ten flags, but the one set of doors seemed only to open from the outside. No one ever came out.

"Nova?" Sitara spoke as the door cracked open. Smiling, Nova saw the baker. Relief flooded her. Unable to stand still, Nova walked toward the back entrance.

Behind the door, a muscular man stood chin up, chest out. The Nomarch's unblinking eyes focused on her. He held a gun to Sitara's head.

"Well, well, well. What do we have here?" At the sound of the Nomarch's voice, Jude began to cry.

III

The Garden

22

Nova's worst fear became a reality. Nomarchs dragged her back to the same river where she had lost her family all those years ago. On the banks of the Odalys River, a gas-masked crowd began to stomp and chant in unison,

> *Great Wheel of Fortune*
> *Turn, Turn, Turn,*
> *Tell Her the Lesson*
> *That She Should Learn*

Drums beat. Light flickered in the people's hands. "Spin it." Nova watched the circular wheel reverberate. Her face contorted. Memories swirled as the wheel rumbled, "Is marriage worth it?" The sound flooded her with memories: the dock, the Outlands, Alister, the kiss, a birth, a boy, a cry—this cry. Nova had difficulty swallowing. Time slowed as the wheel drummed to a stop. Nova's whole body trembled.

"Five," Officer Shaw barked the result. "We now sentence your son to be dipped in a mixture of sulfur and lime. Light him like a torch!" Elation warmed the atmosphere of the mob.

"Stop!" Nova pleaded. "Please. Please!" Her eyes filled as she stared into the eyes of her only son. "Please." Nova cried with all the zeal of a mother—for him to live and make it. Ignoring her pleas, two Nomarchs tied her baby to a post. Like a coiled snake, the rope wrapped itself around him. Jude's square mouth howled.

"Let me die instead," Nova screamed. Lights flickered on and off in the buildings behind them. Marjorie Shaw turned around to look. Faint red lines surged across the ground, illuminating radiation barriers.

"The radiation is rising!" Officer Shaw yelled. The baby whimpered and complained until his face beat red. He couldn't catch his breath.

"Everyone get inside!" Shaw shouted. Before anyone could move, the people's torches flickered. The flames in their hands ignited radiation barriers at their feet, surrounding them all.

Nova searched for a way to free her son, but the red lines surrounded her, too. Before her, the Odalys River sparked, becoming a sea of flames. Like gas meeting fire, it raged. Flames flowed up the riverbanks like a tide, splashing against the shore. Smoke chased close behind. Ash floated, still burning. Pieces of grass and bits of leaves rose in a flame spiral before they lightly rained down to earth. A wave rippled around the fire. The foundation of the city tremored.

The crowd choked on the acid smell as a blanket of smoke covered them. Nova's lungs burned. The riot turned to mass hysteria. Feet ran and trampled. Hands shoved. As many crossed over radiation barriers, mouths gasped in suffocation.

"Nova!" from the confusion came a robotic-sounding voice. A gas mask covered the man's face. "Go!" Alister's voice vibrated like an insect emerging from the underground. "Get to the underground!" Fire and sulfur rained like ash.

Alister's knife cut the ropes, freeing his son from the pole. A Nomarch stepped over the red line to stop him. The radiation barrier spit out electromagnetic waves. Boils formed on the Nomarch's arms, burning. The other Nomarchs stopped at the line. Each border produced a heat wave, forcing the red light to charge out.

"Go!" Alister shouted at Nova again. "Get in the sewer." Nova ran.

"Stop them!" Officer Shaw screamed, racing forward. Nova reached the open drainage grate and rappelled into the underground. The smell was revolting.

The air pressure changed. A rumbling noise came, and a wave blasted. People above ground covered their ears. The flash of light was so bright the Nomarchs' eyes transformed into a live X-ray. They could see everything inside their fellow soldiers. The bones of every skeleton were stunned. The radiation blast hit. More boils formed. One by one, the Nomarchs retched.

The radiation damaged eardrums. Lungs burned. Several slumped to the ground.

The long compression of the radioactive blast released a fireball and sent a destructive wind over the city. The reinforced steel buildings, the Legacy Hall, Valley of the Kings Railway station, and Eliora's public library all crumbled. The dome cracked and splintered. Shards fell to the ground. Flying debris swirled. Material from the west wall flats piled up until nothing inside was recognizable. Every building dropped to its knees. Every monument fell on its face. Even the Vizier, knowing defeat had come, looked for quick relief in the Ensor Estate. There were no survivors above ground.

In a dark tunnel underground, Gwyn's iodine shots flowed through Nova's veins. Despite the earthshaking blast, Jude found safety in his mother's arms. Alister threw a gas mask to his wife and fixed one on his son. Grabbing a flashlight, Alister led the march through water and waste. They raced through the concrete circular tube. Nova's feet splashed in three inches of water as she followed Alister, turning several corners. They weaved through the underground sewer system, tracing the marks that led to the Ensor Gardens.

23

"Four minutes," Alister shouted.

"Stop!" Officer Shaw appeared, running behind them in the sewer, coughing. Another Nomarch stopped to hurl in the tunnel. It echoed through the long tunnel. Crossing the radiation barrier was too much, and he slumped.

"Three minutes until the hour of the lily," Alister said. Nova ran with all her might.

***

"Emmanuel," Are you here?" Alister yelled.

"Emma!" Nova echoed. Brown squinting eyes appeared from the shadows.

"Help me pull this grate. It's lodged," Emma said. Alister's fist pounded the drain above. Gripping the grate, Alister pushed. Emma beat it. Alister pressed the steel outer rim. The creaky grate popped open, and Emma scurried up and held her arms out to pull Nova's baby up.

"You next." Alister hoisted Nova. Out of the corner of her eye, Nova saw the Glistening Tree under a layer of ash. Closing in, Officer Shaw splashed through the water to reach the drainage grate as Alister escaped. The

Glistening Tree's branches hung down, and one lily stood amid the flower clock blooming—only seven more paces. Nova imagined bending through the narrow door and getting Jude to safety.

Lowering her head and bending her knees, she, too, would find security—five more paces. Usually, the light from the Glistening Tree illuminated nearby pathways, flowers, bushes, and even a tiny bubbling stream flowing toward a waterfall. Still, everything hid under a gray layer of ashes—two more paces. The couple stood at the foot of the Glistening Tree. Alister reached into the lily's petals and plucked out the crystal key. He pushed it into the knob.

"Stop!" Officer Shaw screamed.

Nova watched the tree's many rings meld with Alister's crystal key lines. It triggered a hatch. The old mechanical iris dilated slowly. Bark slid into the sides of the tree, and a small door opened.

"Come on." Alister reached for Nova, helping her get inside the Glistening Tree. Alister jumped in, and Emma held the boy out to his father. Alister reached for him as Officer Shaw drew her gun. Marjorie's arms boiled up, and her vision blurred. She pulled the trigger just as the radiation ate through her skin. Emma maneuvered herself in front of the door— pap- pap, ka–ka–ka. Nova heard the gun and watched Emma fight to stand. She stood for a minute longer to shield the family. Nova couldn't stop looking at Emma. The bullet pierced her petite body. Like a small wounded animal, she fell. Silently, Emma curled up and slumped to the floor.

Everything went silent. Nova's ears rang. "Emma!" she screamed. The tree's door closed without warning. Emma lay on the other side.

24

The gun's bullet shell became a key that locked The Glistening Tree's door shut and kept the little family safe inside. The light flickered orange and yellow through the half-moon window at the top of The Glistening Tree's wooden door. A crest of swords in the window guarded her sight against the last bit of the Ensor Gardens.

The tree was no fortified castle. No moat encircled them. No signet rings decorated their fingers, yet they were a family. Like underground rats, the little family saw every door and window close, and Alister instructed them to get as low as possible. Together, they prayed the radioactive materials outside the tree would keep them safe. Iodine surged through the family, protecting them from the Red Death. The family stayed underground for several days, letting the radiation wear off. After the explosion, plants and trees lay under gray dust. A pile of rubble lay where the ceremony once took place. Everything in Eliora was gray—the bodies, the garden, and even the night sky. The whole city rested on its knees—but the boy who survived the Tolerance Law—his eyes opened. His heart beat in his chest. He opened his tiny fist, still holding the crystal key his father had given him. It radiated its protective power.

On the third morning, orange light flickered to life in a leaf on the glistening tree—another leaf pulsed and beamed yellow. The tree breathed, and an orange color surged through the branches to every leaf. The tree drank in the radiation and pulsed with light and life. The tree pulled the surrounding gray into its bark, and its orange color spilled over the city and wasteland.

***

Alister's crystal key opened the door from the underground city, and light burst out. The tree's door dilated. The ashen Ensor Gardens transformed before the family's eyes. A deep red colored the roses. The lilies rose from the ashes and stood tall. The flower clock bloomed. As life and color returned to the Eliora, evergreens swayed in the Ensor Gardens. The sky above The Fractal City turned a bright blue. The sun shone so brightly that it was as if the streets were golden.

One by one, the family stepped out of the root cellar into the light of day. Like rats coming up from underground, the Outlanders of Eliora became like a handful of stars thrown into a dark sky. Baby Jude played sweetly on their union gift quilt in the Ensor Gardens and held the crystal key in his chubby hands.

Emma's body lay ashen on the ground. "Grab her other arm," Alister said. Nova grabbed her arms and, together with her husband, dragged Emma to the base of the Glistening Tree.

The tree was alive. It consumed the radiation in Emma's body. The Glistening Tree pulled the orange and red color out of her and into itself. The Red Death left Emma's body, traveling into the tree's veins. The leaves pulsed and sparked with light.

"Grab the iodine," Alister said, pointing to the door. Nova grabbed it from inside the tree. She injected it into Emma's arm. The boils on Emma's arms healed. Her flesh smoothed over. Her lungs filled with air. She gulped in a breath, and her eyes opened.

"Emma," Nova cried and hugged her friend. She tilted her head back, tears streaming as she yelled. Alister jumped up, pumping his fist in the air. The couple clenched their hands above their heads and let out a roar of joy.

The couple moved Emma into a room prepared for her in the roots of The Glistening Tree. While Emma rested safely in the tree, the couple began to search for other fallen Outlanders. One by one, the little family found people and dragged them to the Glistening Tree, which continued to pull radiation into itself. Alister and Nova injected each fallen Outlander with iodine. Joy filled each Outlander's heart as their boils from the plague healed, flesh smoothed over, and their dead lungs filled with air.

When every Outlander had been woken up, the family stood before the Glistening Tree, smiling. Alister had plans to build the underground root city. Nova helped each Outlander find a room in the roots.

Above them, the Glistening Tree's light, glowing like a comet, soared toward the sun, passing by the Earth. Its dust trail could light up a thousand stories, highlighting a thousand souls that passed away. The dust molded and displayed a perfect masterpiece. It formed a perfect line, a lineage, a work of art—like an arrow pointing north. The tree stood like a lighthouse to the lost at sea— a torch to those bound in the rubble. Jude, who survived the Tolerance Law, turned the world upside down, becoming a boy between two worlds.

25

Months later...

The underground root city welcomed the most unlikely of people. Outlanders of every kind came to the long dining hall table with the story of how they had come to live in The Glistening Tree after the blast destroyed The Fractal City of Eliora.

Fine linen and a table runner covered the long table in the dining hall. Place cards with each Outlander's name marked their spot at the table. Each setting had a charger, plate, glass, and silverware. Baskets of bread and bottles of wine sat on the table. Roses, lilies, greenery, and an assortment of flowers bloomed over glass vases.

"They grabbed my arms and dragged me to the tree," one Outlander whispered at the table. "The next thing I knew, I felt this pull, and the radiation left my body. My eyes opened up, and I could breathe again."

"I was buried in rubble," the baker commented Sitara. "I felt the blast in the city and fell through the floor of Second Street Bakery into a dark pit. I went unconscious. Like you, I came alive at the base of The Glistening Tree."

"Did Alister bring you to a room in the root city?" the Outlander asked.

"Yes, he carried me into the tree, but as soon as I went through the door, the wounds on my legs healed. The boils on my arms cleared up. I could walk. I followed him down the stairs to one of the many rooms he built into the roots. You should have seen it. Everybody was laughing and smiling."

"It was the same for me. People hugged, cried, and shouted—welcome home. It was like the darkness had left the world, and I lived in the light of the sun."

"He also gave me a job—a job I love," Sitara said, smiling.

"Me too! After living in the Outlands, I couldn't image work being fun. But I love it. It's like I was made for this."

"Do you know what will happen to the city?" Sitara asked, readjusting herself in her seat.

"Alister is rebuilding. He is making all things new up there. The Tree is drinking in the radiation, and he'll rebuild it over time."The Glistening Tree's orange glow lit the underground city.

Jude, the first boy to survive The Tolerance Law, finally lived among his own people. The double doors opened at the back of the dining hall. A baby sat in a wagon. Emma pulled him forward. The sound of a baby cooing brought oo's and ah's from the people.

"A boy. A real boy!" an Outlander whispered.

"And out in the open, too! He's not hiding from anyone. I never thought I'd see the day," a little old woman said, slapping her knee and smiling.

The room fell silent, and a hush fell over the crowd at the table. The piano started singing beautiful notes, and Gwyn played with clear vision. Carson stood at the front of the stage at the head of the room. He held a black book in his right hand.

The back double doors reopened. Every head turned from waiting. A woman in a white dress appeared for the public ceremony of her marriage that had secretly taken place a year earlier. The joyful feeling of romance filled the big hall as the violin created harmony with the piano. The smell of sweet-scented pine filled the dining hall where roots intertwined. Nova wore her hair half up, half down. Blonde curls fell down her back. Her white smile widened when she saw her groom at the front of the church; no nerves this time, only joy.

Alister beamed like the sun. Tears of joy streamed down his face as he laughed and cried all at the same time. The smiling groom wiped tears from his eyes. His bride came to him in front of a host of people. No more hiding. No more waiting. She was here. The time was now.

The smell of roses filled the air. The rhythm of each step closed. Lace and fine linen trailed behind Nova as she solemnly marched to meet the love of her life. Together, the couple turned to face the altar. The priest read from the Psalter. Soft light peaked through the stained glass windows on the side of Thorncrown dining hall. Emma smiled at the head of the table, bouncing Jude up and down on her knee. Face to face, the couple's love crescendoed. All that is left in the story is for the groom to lift the veil.

The End

Acknowledgments

A big thanks to you, dear reader; no one owes me a read. Thank you for picking up these pages.

My Savior—
Jesus, the most excellent storyteller of all. You made, saved, and sustain me. It is a joy to worship you.

My Family—
Mark Baker, thank you for your steadfast love and kindness. Thanks for being my first reader. I love you (and your editing skills).
My five children: Thank you, Elias, Owen, Eleanor, Alister, and Atticus, for being the best kids a mom could hope for. I love you more than you know.
Sara Baker, thank you for editing for me and offering such valuable feedback. Your comments created so many light bulb moments for me.
David Park, thank you for never being too busy to call. Your creative insights, book recommendations, historical knowledge, and creative deadlines kept me writing.
Dani Bruno, you are the biggest encourager. Thank you for lifting people up and so generously encouraging others.
Dave and Grace Park, I love learning, reading, and writing because of you. Thank you for sparking my love for creativity.

The Order of Saint Tumnus—my writing group.

Mark Baker,

Devon Tarr, thank you for encouraging me to express my emotions through writing. Your counsel, friendship, and love for Jesus have marked me.

Nathan Tarr, your sermons set my imagination on fire for over a decade. Hebrews 11:23 inspired the first idea for this book; thank you.

My friends—

Lauren Perkins and Alyssa Laing, thank you for always encouraging me. It's nice to know we are only one Marco Pollo away.

Becky Hatfield and Chelsea Zimmerman, I can't wait to be old ladies in a retirement home together. Maybe it will be like college when we laughed about nothing for two straight hours.

Lauren Mefford, thank you for chatting with me at the beach about this story and for sharing your nursing expertise.

My Texas living room writing group— Rachel, Kaylie, Christie, Brooke, and Rachel H.—you ladies are so creative. Thank you for reading my earliest manuscripts and taking the time to give such valuable feedback; I am so grateful.

How could I leave without mentioning my pets?

My dogs: Luna and Penny, so many ideas came to me while walking these pups around the pond.

My cats: Nova, Cheddar Biscuit, and Mowgli, special shoutout to the best late-night writing companions; I love their furry faces.

Made in the USA
Columbia, SC
14 January 2025